1/19/23

Dear Esther,

I hope you
enjoy my first fiction
novel written with my
friend Leslie Lynn.

Thank you for
your friendship and being
my buddy at pilates!

With love,

Gina Fromang

The Oasis

The Oasis
Book One of the Oasis Series

By Noel Lynn

Published in the United States of America,
Branford, Florida
First Edition

Library of Congress Control Number: 2022921314
ISBN Paperback: 9798361675838

Cover Art by Karen LeMonnier
Karen's style is inspired by the Impressionist artists and directly from nature. Her art can be seen in galleries and shows throughout Florida. Her paintings focus on the beautiful rivers and landscapes of North Florida which is the setting for this book.
Contact her at lemons50@icloud.com

Dedication

From its fortuitous beginning to its precipitous conclusion everything that led to the manifestation of this book has had the hand of God upon it. Therefore, it is with a humble and grateful heart that this book is dedicated to our Lord and Savior, Jesus Christ.

Table of Contents

Chapter One

"When you pass through the waters, I will be with you, and when you pass through the rivers, they will not sweep over you. When you walk through the fire, you will not be burned; the flames will not set you ablaze." Isaiah 43:2

The lime rock road into the Oasis was long and dusty. The white clouds billowing up behind her gave her a sense of comfort that whatever she was running from couldn't follow her there. Miami's loud sounds and chaotic scenes seemed to be in the distant past now as the road opened up before her. She needed a new beginning, and now that she was there, she sensed that nothing would ever be the same again.

The road narrowed and bent gracefully to the right. Suddenly, the dusty road was gone, and her Jeep entered a beautiful, tree-shaded lane. The giant live oaks that formed the canopy above her stood tall and majestic, and the air beneath them felt instantly cool. She passed a small, discreet wooden sign that said *The Oasis,* and she knew she was headed the right way. The road wound its way through the canopy as she kept a sharp eye for a road on the right that would be her turn. Now and then, the trees would open up, and she would glimpse the river, glistening in the midday Florida sun, its reflections sparkling like diamonds. She spotted the obscure turn-off and had to brake hard not to miss it, its entrance barely wide enough for her Jeep. She pulled in and stopped, reluctant to drive into an abandoned place. On the ground were remnants of an old mailbox, its post rotted and scattered in pieces. The box was crushed flat, and she could see a hand-painted red cardinal and a small inscription that read, *Almost Heaven.*

She made her way down the narrow path as the overgrowth brushed heavily along the sides of her Jeep. It was evident that no one had been there in a long time. After a short drive in, the brush fell away and opened up into a cleared but overgrown property. She could see the little cracker-style cabin ahead of her and the moving waters of the river behind it. She parked behind the house and gazed at what would be her new home. She was still surprised at herself for buying the place sight unseen. Though she'd seen pictures of the property, nothing could have prepared her for the beauty of the place. She knew she shouldn't have been so impulsive but needed to do something and not analyze it for days. Now, as she gazed at her surroundings, she was sure she had done the right thing.

She found the key exactly where the realtor had told her it would be hidden, up over the door on the ledge of the door frame. It slipped easily into the lock, but the knob was hard to turn, and the door seemed stuck. She turned her shoulder into the door and gave it a mighty shove, but it didn't budge. She tried again, and on the third try, the door unexpectedly flew open, launching her onto the floor in a cloud of dust. She sat for a moment, then slowly hauled herself to her feet. Looking around through the haze, she didn't know whether to laugh or cry. By the cobwebs, the furniture coverings, and the grimy windows, she could tell it had been a long time since anyone had lived there. Knowing she would spend the night there motivated her, and she went to work.

The sunrise dawned a brilliant yellow-orange in the eastern sky, and from her cozy little rocker on the front porch, she realized she had never even inquired about the details of the place. The surprise of the perfect sunrise told her there was much to discover about her new home. She watched, almost mesmerized, as an osprey circled over the shimmering water, then landed in one of the towering cypress trees lining the bank in front of the cabin.

She had stayed up late trying to put some order to the place and had spent a restless night wondering what might be crawling about in the old house. She had gotten the bedroom in decent shape and was thankful she had brought fresh sheets, pillows, and a quilt. The old bed, while creaky, was comfortable, but she had not gotten any deep sleep. She was now thankful for the hot cup of coffee in her hand and her last-minute impulse to pack a coffee maker and supplies.

She had brought little with her as the realtor told her the place came furnished. Most of her things were in storage in Miami. She wondered why she hadn't moved everything with her. She also hadn't given up her condo on Brickell, though it was empty and ready for sale or lease. As brave as it was to come here, by herself, surroundings unknown, she was still keeping an ace in the hole.

As she sat gazing at the river, now that she finally had a quiet moment to stop and think about things, it occurred to her, for the first time, that she was all alone in an unfamiliar place. The stark realization of her predicament brought a flow of unexpected tears. She didn't realize she had been holding in all her suffering and pain. She'd learned to be strong and fearless, and she didn't understand any other way.

As she watched the river winding its way past her, its extraordinary beauty struck her. In the throes of her loss and pain, she had moved on a whim, and she hadn't thought it through. But, now that she was here, somehow, it seemed to fit her. At thirty-five, she felt oddly at home for the first time.

The old, rustic river cabin needed much more work than she'd realized, and she had to quell the overwhelming feelings rising inside her. She couldn't afford to buckle now; she would need to pull together whatever inner strength she had. She was alone in this world and it was up to her, and her alone, to put together this new life.

She felt the sweat trickle down her back as she hauled the downed limbs in the yard into a large pile at the back of the property. Though accustomed to the heat of South Florida, North Florida had humidity new to her. She'd been giving the house her full attention for the last few days, but she desperately wanted to see what the property would look like without all the overgrowth and debris. Besides, she needed the physical labor to blow off some of the emotional steam building since she arrived. She was taking a trip into town a little later and thought she might inquire about having someone mow the property. Even a rough job would be a significant improvement.

Back inside, she stripped off her sticky, sweaty work clothes and hopped in the shower. She hadn't figured out the hot water yet, so she stood shivering under the weak stream of cold water. The property had a well, apparently a deep one, stretching into the 72-degree aquifer that ran in intricate pathways under this part of Florida. She had read about the abundant and beautiful springs that dotted North Florida, but she had never seen or experienced them. Something she would need to add to her list of things to do.

Her mind was preoccupied with everything she needed to do when she got to town as she drove her Jeep down the overgrown lane leading to the dirt road. It was slow going again, the high brush making it difficult to navigate out of her property. As she got to the turn, she pulled out, rolling slowly, to see if the way was clear. Suddenly, she heard a loud truck horn and the sound of tires sliding on gravel. She snapped out of her daydreaming just in time to brake hard to avoid a collision with a pick-up truck, their bumpers stopping within inches of each other. She sat for a moment, her heart pounding in her chest, her hands still gripping the steering wheel like a vice. Through the cloud of dust stirred up in the skirmish, she saw the truck's driver-side door open and someone step out. She didn't move but instead braced herself for whatever was going to happen. As a city girl, her instincts were to reach for the gun under her seat, but something told her that wasn't necessary here. As he approached her window, she could see him more clearly now. Though he was a large, intimidating man, his expression wasn't an angry one. She thought she detected a slight smile as he pushed his ball cap back on his head.

"You ok, ma'am?" he said in a soft, Southern accent.

She sighed deeply and pressed her forehead against the steering wheel of the Jeep in obvious embarrassment. She could only nod as she could not turn and meet his gaze. Instead, she reached for the handle of her car door, slowly opened it, and swung herself around. When she finally dared to look at him, she saw only kindness and concern in his eyes.

"I-I'm sorry!" she stuttered, "I've just gotten here and haven't had a chance to clear all this away from my driveway. I didn't see you!"

"It's ok," he said, "no harm done. You just buy this place?"

"Yes, I just arrived a few days ago. The place is pretty overgrown. It doesn't look like anyone has lived here in a long time. I hope to find someone to help me get the property at least mowed. Would you happen to know someone?" she asked.

"I'm Gabe," he said with a chuckle," Gabe Barrett."

"Oh!" she said, embarrassed by her lack of manners." I'm Ko - I mean, Kennedy!" She'd almost blurted out her childhood nickname of Koko, given her by her father as a child. She decided in this new life, she wanted people to know her by her given name of Kennedy. These people here seemed too down to earth to take a city girl named Koko seriously. Besides, her heart needed to leave some memories behind, at least for a while.

They shook hands, and he smiled at her. It was the first chance she'd had to look at him. He had a kind nature that she was sure of, but he was an imposing guy. He was tall, probably six-foot-four or better, and she could see by his build he was strong. She noticed that his hands were rough, his jeans were worn, and he had a capable air. He was a man who worked hard for a living. She felt an instant trust odd for her suspicious nature. Through her career and upbringing, she had been conditioned to view everyone with skepticism, at least upon a first meeting.

He seemed at ease with himself. Something her dad had always described as "being comfortable in your own skin." He moved in an easy-going, almost graceful manner as he walked over to survey the driveway into her property.

"Well, you're right. No one has been here for a long while. Not since Mr. Willer passed, I think, and that's been a few years," he said as he stood staring at the overgrown lane and rubbing his chin. "Listen, I've got a tractor and a bush hog. I'll come up here later today and get this taken care of for you."

Her heart lifted a bit that she might make some progress on getting the property in shape. Getting her driveway in order was a good first step. She thought to protest for a brief second but realized his matter-of-fact tone left no room for argument. She was taken aback by his take-charge attitude; she wasn't used to others making decisions for her. She had great pride in her self-sufficiency and independence.

"What will you charge me?" she asked, but he said nothing, gave her a wave of his hand as he yanked the truck door open and climbed in, his motions effortless. She watched as he drove away.

She climbed back into the Jeep and started down the dirt road toward town and noticed she felt off-kilter. Maybe it was the adrenaline of the near miss, but she had an odd feeling in her gut. It was a feeling she was unaccustomed to, and she couldn't quite put her finger on it. It slowly came to her that this man, who she didn't even know, made her feel safe. It was not what she expected, and she wondered why this feeling felt so foreign to her.

She wasn't used to driving on the backcountry roads and was unfamiliar with the lack of traffic and congestion. She realized she'd been daydreaming again when she slightly swerved onto the shoulder. She would need to pay more attention while driving around these narrow roads. Fortunately, there was no activity on the road and no signs of the inhabitants of the farmhouses that dotted the fields on either side.

The closest town was a twenty-minute drive from her cabin. On the way, she wondered about the former owners of the place and who had made the mailbox. She was also curious about the name of the neighborhood, the Oasis. She set those questions aside and focused on her town visit and the supplies she needed. She would have to find a hardware store, a grocery store, and something for lunch. She had had nothing to eat of substance in the last few days other than the few snacks and packaged items she had brought from Miami.

She planned to stop at the hardware store first, but her hunger was getting the best of her. She figured there probably weren't any Cuban cafes nearby like those within walking distance of her Miami condominium on Brickell. She would miss her daily cafe con leche and her weekly indulgence on Sundays of a Cuban sandwich with a side of black beans. Her favorite Cuban cafe was down the street from her condominium and in the lobby of the building that housed the international law firm office where she had worked since graduating from law school. She always enjoyed this simple comfort meal to give her fuel for working all afternoon and sometimes well into the evening on Sundays to get a jump start on her busy weeks. She passed a restaurant that, by the looks of the cars outside, was a local favorite, so she made a fast U-turn and pulled into Fancy's Country Kitchen. She parked the Jeep beside the slew of mostly pick-up trucks in the gravel lot and headed inside.

She realized there was nothing fancy about Fancy's. The restaurant had a crowd of older couples, groups of men in construction clothes, and families with young children. Inside there were twenty worn wooden tables with a smattering of mismatched chairs. The walls were pale yellow and covered with pictures of the local sports teams and of the little town in days gone by. Everything in the place was a little shabby, but it looked clean, and the smell of something delicious cooking in the kitchen made her mouth water.

She was used to heads turning when she walked into a room, but this was different. It seemed everyone in the place stopped talking and looked her way when she walked in. After a long and quiet moment, a waitress yelled to her to take a seat anywhere.

She found an open table in the corner, and the other patrons finally seemed to lose interest in her and returned to their conversations. She figured the restaurant was a local town hangout with a clientele of regulars. She was a stranger to them and didn't look like she belonged in the place.

She was handed a plastic menu by a boy who could not have been older than eleven or twelve. He was awkward as he set down a glass of water and told her someone would be right with her. Soon after, the waitress made it to her table and paused with a pen and pad.

" Do you know what you want, honey?" she asked as she tapped her pen impatiently on her pad. She was a busy woman, as Kennedy noticed there didn't seem any other waitresses around. "You're a new face, just passing through?"

"Actually, I've just moved to the area," Kennedy said as she perused the menu. She was always cautious about giving strangers too much information about herself, so she left it at that. "I'll have the pulled pork sandwich plate and an iced tea, unsweet, please."

The waitress scratched down her order and bustled off.

Kennedy was tall, standing at almost six feet without shoes. In her city life, though, she usually wore high heels, as she liked to command attention, especially at work. Her physique was fine-boned, long-legged, slender, and very striking. She looked like a model, but her presence carried a more serious tone. Her skin was fair, and she had a sprinkling of freckles across her nose, giving away her black Irish descent. It showed in her light skin tone and delicate features; she had a broad smile, perfect teeth, and a sculptured chin. Her hair was waist long, dark brown, almost black, and she wore it in a high ponytail most days. It was thick like a horse's mane and had natural waves when she didn't painstakingly blow dry it straight.

Her eyes were large, blue-green, and were wide-set on her face. You would have noticed them without her hair pulled back, but with it away from her face, you were immediately drawn to them. They were crystal clear and unusual, and her father had always described them as *sparkling eyes that danced.* As beautiful as she was, her eyes were her trademark feature. For years, men had crossed rooms to introduce themselves to her and to ask *are they real?*

The homemade Southern fare was comforting and delicious, and she was happy she had stopped at the little place. The waitress checked on her and dropped her tab on the table. She paid her bill and walked out of the restaurant with a swift gait. It was not the time to think about any awkwardness she may have felt; she had a million and one things to do. She was ready to tackle her to-do list.

The hardware store was only a couple of blocks from the restaurant, so finding it was easy. Kennedy parked right in front and thought how effortless it seemed to get around in the country. City life had always made things like finding a parking space an ordeal. She was coming around to a slower pace, though she could not entirely shake the hustle and hurry of the big city. She still felt that sense of urgency running through her veins and suspected it would probably take a while for that to go away.

Her list was long, and she didn't know where to start. Being unfamiliar with the store didn't help, so she wandered around to get the lay of the land. She decided she would start by trying to address the lock on her front door and the stickiness of the door itself. City girls were conditioned to ensure they had secure doors; hers was anything but. As she stood in the aisle looking over all the locks and door parts, hand on her chin, she heard a voice behind her.

"Whatcha 'frettin 'about, darlin'?"

She turned to see who this person was and was surprised to see a tall, dapper, country gentleman dressed in a pair of khaki slacks, a plaid short-sleeved buttoned-down shirt, and a fedora hat with a feather tucked into the band. She opened her mouth to respond, but nothing came out. She wasn't used to strangers being so familiar with her. When he noticed her reaction, he shuffled his feet and broke into a broad and engaging smile. She couldn't help but smile back.

"I-I'm looking for a lock for my door," she stuttered." Do you work here?"

"Nooo," he chuckled, "but I do know my way around a little bit. What kind of lock do you need?" he asked, his eyes darting up and down the aisle.

"I have no idea!" she said, waving her hands and her list around in the air. "I've just bought this old place, and it needs so much work! I don't even know where to start."

"I'm Bobby Finn," he said. "But everyone around here just calls me Finn. Can I see that?" he said, tentatively pointing to her list.

"Oh yes, I-I'm sorry, I'm Kennedy!" she said as she handed him her list. Again, she was embarrassed by her lack of decorum. It wasn't like her. She was raised with impeccable manners, but something about these friendly, country people threw her off balance. She realized she moved and thought at a different pace than these nice people and probably needed to slow down. Otherwise, she would seem rude, which was not a good impression to make on the people coming into her new life.

Bobby Finn was studying her list and rubbing his chin. He was quite an interesting character, she thought. He was not a big man, per se, but he was tall, probably standing over six feet, and had a relaxed and capable air about him. He had a head of brilliant white hair and bright blue eyes that sparkled with amusement when he talked. His slow, Southern drawl and cheery demeanor put her at ease, and she could tell he had a funny way about him and probably a delightful sense of humor. She guessed his age to be somewhere around seventy.

"Well, Kennedy, you have quite the list here. Are you planning on doing all this work yourself? It seems you don't need a list; you need a contractor," he said with a chuckle. "Where is this house of yours? Close by?"

"It's about twenty minutes from here. I live out in the Oasis." She was unsure why she told a perfect stranger so much about herself but felt comfortable with it. She was a good judge of character. She knew she had nothing to fear from Bobby Finn.

"Well, then, Kennedy, it seems we are neighbors! How about that?" he said, throwing his head back with a laugh. His laugh was contagious, and she giggled a little. "Now come on darlin', let's see what we can do about this list."

After she and Finn spent nearly an hour shopping and loading the bags in the Jeep, she hit the grocery store and started home, her mood light-hearted for the first time in a while. They had had fun doing what she had dreaded and thought would be a miserable and stressful task. Somehow in that short time, they had become fast friends and promised to see each other again soon. From his description of where he lived, it seemed he was just down the road from her place. Since she had ventured no further into the Oasis past her turn-off, she had no idea where that might be but thought it would be easy to find.

She turned off the lime rock road onto the tree-shaded lane and slowed so she wouldn't miss her turn-off. Ahead she saw the easement was mowed in front of her property along with the driveway to the house. She stopped and looked for the mailbox, but it was gone. Her heart sank a little as she had hoped to preserve it somehow. Driving down to the house was easy now; the brush cut way back off the road on either side. When she reached the clearing, she realized that the whole property had been perfectly groomed. The remaining limbs had been gathered into the pile, which was now a smoldering pile of ash, and the high grass had been cut into perfect stripes. She could hardly believe her eyes and felt overwhelmed by the kindness shown to her by these people who barely knew her. How would she ever be able to return that kindness? What did she have to give back?

She parked the Jeep close to the door so she wouldn't have to carry all the supplies from the hardware store and the groceries too far. She unloaded the groceries first in case she ran out of steam.

She could always get the supplies later. When she stepped onto the back porch, something on the little table near the door caught her eye. It was the mailbox propped up carefully against the old oil lamp that stood there. The tears came over her with a flood of emotions. She felt happy but sad at the same time, the mix of emotions causing her knees to buckle, and she sat down hard on the front step. She put her face in her hands and let the tears flow for the second time in a matter of days. She realized she hadn't really cried in years.

The setting sun, mirrored in the flowing river, reflected shades of pink and gold. A myriad of rose and salmon hues were blanketing the giant live oaks and cypress trees that lined her property close to the river's edge. She sat on the porch with a glass of wine and tried to enjoy the view without intruding thoughts.

Her Miami condominium on Brickell had sweeping unobstructed views of Biscayne Bay, but she had never been home to enjoy it. She had worked 80-90 hours a week in the law firm to keep up with the billing amount required. When she became the youngest partner five years ago at age thirty, the work hadn't slowed down; her responsibilities had increased. She was like a hamster on a spinning wheel; the grind never ended.

River living would be different. This rural North Florida county was a long way from the craziness of Dade County. South Florida seemed like a world away as she sipped her wine and took in the natural beauty surrounding her cabin. The deer had come out of the woods and were grazing on the grass near the river's edge. She watched as now and then, they would lift their heads to gaze at her. The picturesque scene felt like food for her wounded soul, and she sensed the mornings and evenings spent here on her porch would go a long way to healing her heart.

She was running, but her feet wouldn't move. She could see the door through the smoke and the flames but couldn't reach it. She could hear voices shouting, calling out in panic, but she couldn't understand what they were saying. She was dying; she knew it. Her lungs were full of smoke. She felt a hand reach out and grabbed it, but it slipped away. She was lost. All was lost.

She was suddenly jolted out of sleep by loud thunder and heavy rain thumping on the metal roof of her cabin. It wasn't the storm that had woken her up, though; she was sure of that. She glanced at the clock on her nightstand and saw it was after three in the morning. Slowly her eyes adjusted to the darkness, but even as she oriented herself, she still couldn't calm her heart or slow her breathing. She switched on the nightlight beside her bed, hoping it would ground her. As she slowly returned to herself, she laid back down and tried to fall back asleep but could not put the visions of the fire and the sounds of the voices out of her mind. When the eastern sky lightened with the dawn, she was still awake, the fear of the dream still lingering.

Chapter Two

"For I know the plans I have for you," declares the LORD, "plans to prosper you and not to harm you, plans to give you hope and a future." Jeremiah 29:11

It was turning into a beautiful late spring morning, and as the sun rose over the river, she felt better, the last remnants of the dream leaving her. There was a slight coolness in the air she knew would not last long before the heat of the day set in. Flashes of light filtered through the trees, their brilliant beams dancing on the water like fireflies. The osprey she had seen before was flying high above the treetops; his neck craned downward, looking for prey in the watery depths of the river below. It was a sight she was sure she would never grow tired of, and she felt the most hope in these quiet morning moments. Hope that someday she would feel whole again. While she knew that would not come without pain, she believed she could get through it.

She had decided that day she would venture into the Oasis to explore her new neighborhood. She wanted to find Finn's place and thank him for all his help at the hardware store and further their friendship. There was something about him she felt connected to though she couldn't put her finger on it. He was an old soul, that was for sure, and she knew herself well enough to know she was one too. Maybe they were just kindred spirits. Whatever the connection was between them, she was just happy to have found a friend.

She hoped Finn could help her find Gabe, who had been so kind to mow her property. She wanted to thank him for all his work, but she had no idea where to look for him. She wasn't even sure he lived there in the Oasis.

Not wanting to show up empty-handed, she baked boxed brownies. She wasn't a cook, so that was the closest she would get to delivering something homemade. Through the years, she never had the time or inclination to learn to cook. She wasn't interested in it with the steady flow of business dinners with clients and the abundance of take-out opportunities in her neighborhood.

With trepidation, she inspected the old gas stove and realized that she would have to light the pilot. Even though she viewed herself as a capable woman, these tasks were foreign to her. She suspected that would be the case with the old water heater, too, so she decided she might as well figure it out. She sighed with relief when she heard the whoosh of the burner igniting in the old stove. She would tackle the water heater a little later.

The smell of the baking brownies gave her a warm feeling inside. The old cabin had grown on her over the last few days. With the cobwebs and dust out of the way, it was quaint, and the old furniture was sturdy and comfortable. She especially liked the big chair by the fireplace. When she got more settled, she hoped to catch up on her reading there.

With two plates of brownies, just in case she found Gabe, she pulled her Jeep out onto the lane. She was again overcome with gratitude for the kindness the people here had shown her. The entrance to her property looked well-groomed like someone lived there now and cared for it. Things seemed to be coming together for her here, and the place was feeling like home.

The lane wound around, following the river, and now and again, she could see the brilliant reflections through the trees. There were no other houses for a while, then slowly, she saw a few tucked away in the trees. Finn had told her she could find him where the road bent hard to the left. She would see his place straight ahead and would know he was home if his old red pickup truck was parked out front.

She spotted the truck and pulled the Jeep slowly down the leaf-covered driveway. The place was quiet, and she sat for a moment listening to the birds chirp and the wind in the trees. Somewhere close by, she could hear someone chopping wood, so she got out of her Jeep and walked around the side of the cabin. She could hear the chickens squawking as they heard her coming, and the sound of someone chopping wood stopped.

"Finn?" she called out to see if she could figure out where he was. She heard him securing the ax in the chopping block and stacking the wood pieces into a pile. As she rounded the back corner of the house, he spotted her and broke into his trademark smile.

"Well, hello darlin' aren't you a sight for sore eyes!" he said in his heavy Southern drawl. He lifted his hat, tipped it toward her, and settled it back down on his head in the true form of a Southern gentleman.

She laughed and held out her plate of brownies. "I've come by to thank you for all your help yesterday. I would probably still be standing in the door lock aisle if it weren't for you."

He took the plate from her, and she saw his eyes light up. "That was mighty nice of you, Kennedy, but completely unnecessary. Shopping with you was the most fun I've had in a while! Come on up on the porch and let me pour you some tea."

She climbed the back steps of his cabin and sat in one of the old comfortable rockers. She could hear Finn rattling around in the kitchen inside the back door. Soon after, he stepped out with a tray that carried two tall glasses of tea with lemon wedges and mint leaves tucked by the rim.

He held the tray out to her, and she gingerly took one. He took his own, set the tray down, then settled into the rocker beside her. They were quiet for a while, sipping their tea and listening to the sounds of the little homestead, the silence between them not at all uncomfortable.

"How's that list of chores coming?" he mused, with a smile, as he looked out over the backyard.

She laughed. "I'm embarrassed to say I haven't accomplished a thing since I saw you last."

"Well, it will still be there tomorrow; I wouldn't fret about it. Frettin 'won't get it done either," he said with a chuckle.

"Yes, I suppose you're right about that. To be honest, I have no idea where to even begin. I'm not the handy type."

"You don't say," he said with a wink.

She laughed again. "I've actually never owned a house before; I've always lived in a condo with a maintenance man."

"I would never have guessed," he said teasing her. "I imagine that old cabin could use a little work. It's been empty for a number of years."

"Yes, it does, and I'm afraid it's probably more than I can handle. It looked a lot more livable in the pictures," she said with a laugh.

"I know somebody who might could help," he said. "He lives here in the Oasis, and he's pretty good at what he does. What do ya say I take you for a ride in my pick-up truck, and let's go see if the old boy is around?"

"Oh, that would be great!" she said. "I'd love to get someone started on the work."

"Well, come on then darlin', he's not far away."

———————

When they rolled up to the property in Finn's old Ford, Kennedy could see a figure working in the field out by a barn. Finn gave a toot of the horn, and the figure waved and started toward them. She got out of the truck and looked around at the old farm. The farmhouse was large and beautiful with white paint, dark brown stained wood on the porches, and emerald green shutters. The front beds were planted with native foliage and bright annuals, and the yard was neatly mowed. The rest of the property, many acres, she guessed, had a smattering of livestock in the fields and a few outbuildings, one of which was the old but restored barn. As the figure approached, she turned to take a look at him.

"Hello, Finn," he said as he removed his work gloves and stuck out his hand.

"Hello, Gabe, I've brought someone to see you. This is…"

"Kennedy," Gabe finished with a slight smile. "Hello, again."

"Y'all already know each other? Well, I'll be damned."

"Well, we've met," Kennedy said. "I'm afraid I almost caused a collision on the lane yesterday. The brush was so overgrown I couldn't see when I was pulling out of my driveway. But thanks to Gabe's quick reflexes…" she trailed off. "Thank you for mowing my property; that was very nice of you."

"You're welcome; it was really no trouble at all," he said with a smile, "anytime."

There was an awkward moment when they all looked at each other. Finn, who had been watching them, threw his hands up in the air and turned to go.

"Since ya'll are already acquainted, I'm going to let you two get on with it. Kennedy here needs a contractor to do some work on her house. I told her you might could help," he said as he waved his hat between them. "Y'all talk about it."

Kennedy smiled. She loved Finn's way. Direct and to the point, just like her. He waved his hat as the old Ford rattled out of the driveway and turned onto the road.

Gabe turned to Kennedy. "So the old place needs some work? I'm not surprised. It's been vacant for a long time."

"Yes," she said. "I don't even know where to begin. I mean, it's livable, but barely." She laughed. "I don't know much about construction, so I can't tell you all it needs. I bought it sight unseen, just from a listing on the Internet."

"Well, that was pretty brave, but I can tell you, you got a great property. I don't know what all you'll need to do to get the house in shape, but there aren't many pieces of land like that left on the river."

"It is beautiful; I actually really love it. And thanks for making me feel better about it," she said as she laughed.

"Well, I have to ask, what makes a girl buy a cabin, sight unseen, and move out here to the woods?"

Her expression clouded, and Gabe was instantly sorry he'd asked the question. She dropped her head, then looked up and out onto the homestead.

" Just needed a change, that's all," she said quietly.

They were silent for a moment as she stared out into the field, her thoughts a thousand miles away.

"Well, how about I come by and look at the house, see what it needs," he said as her eyes slowly returned to him.

"That would be great; I'm around almost anytime."

"Tomorrow morning, ok? Say ten o'clock?" he asked.

"Yes, that's fine, I'll be there."

"Ok, then I'll see you tomorrow," he said as he turned to go but realized she had no car and no way to get home. It was too far to walk. "Hey, where's your car?"

"Oh," she said. "I rode down here with Finn. My Jeep is back at his place. I'll just walk down there. It's not too far."

Gabe looked at his watch and noticed it was nearing the hottest part of the day, then at Kennedy's lightly clad feet. "It's farther than you think. Are you going to trek down the dirt road in those?" he said, pointing to her white sandals.

"Oh," she said as she looked down at her feet and then at the road.

"Come on," he said. "I'll run you down there in the truck."

———————————

When he dropped her off at the Jeep, there was no sign of Finn, and his red truck was gone. She climbed in and headed for home. As she was making her way there, she noticed a beautiful, old tobacco barn set back off the road and a hand-carved sign that read "The Pavilion." She wondered what that might be and made a mental note to ask Finn about it the next time she saw him. Whatever it was, it was lovingly cared for; that was evident. She realized, with regret, she hadn't delivered Gabe's brownies. She thought about heading back over but decided that might be awkward. She would just give them to him tomorrow when he came by.

She liked her new surroundings. She thought about the life she left back in Miami and couldn't think of a thing she missed. Her hectic, busy life in Miami was all she had ever known, but now that she had experienced the quiet beauty of river life, she didn't think she could ever live in the city again. When she left Miami, she was running from the memories and didn't care where she ended up. Now that she was here, she realized how lucky she had been to find her way to this place.

She spent the rest of the day putting things in order as best she could. She piled all the things Finn had helped her find at the hardware store in the corner as she laughed to herself. She guessed she would turn those over to Gabe and realized she had been kidding herself thinking she could get any of that stuff done. She could barely turn a screwdriver if she were honest about it.

She was looking forward to Gabe coming over and giving her an assessment of the house, and she was excited about the prospect of fixing up the old place. Upon her arrival, she had been discouraged by the cabin's condition, but now she thought a project was just what she needed. Something interesting and rewarding to focus on would give her mind and soul a much-needed distraction. When she crawled into her creaky old bed, she settled in quickly and fell right to sleep. It was a peaceful sleep, the first one in a while.

———————

Gabe arrived at ten o'clock sharp the next morning, as promised. She had brewed a fresh pot of coffee, so she would have something to offer him along with a pitcher of iced tea. She had never been much of a tea drinker, but the memory of Finn's lemon-mint sweet tea still lingered. So much so that she had made a quick dash that morning to the country store, not far from the cabin, to get some tea bags. While hers was not nearly as delicate and refined as Finn's, she decided it was good for a first attempt.

As Gabe wandered around the house inspecting beams and making notes, Kennedy watched him work. She was intrigued by how he moved and wondered how a man of his size was so graceful. His sandy-colored hair had no hint of gray, not even in the temples where most men turned. She figured they must be of similar age though he had the beginning signs of some crow's feet around his eyes. She suspected that was not from age but rather from working long hours outside in the Florida sun. She hadn't noticed his eyes the first time they met, but she did at their second encounter. They were a soft cornflower blue that reflected his obvious gentle manner. When he'd asked about her reasons for moving to the Oasis, his eyes had a seemingly sympathetic sadness even though he could not have possibly known why she was there. She could see by his broad shoulders and trim waist he was fit. Even though he had a defined and sturdy form, she could tell it was not built in a gym. No, this man worked hard for a living; his build was the result of blood and sweat.

"This old place is in surprisingly good shape, structurally," he said, looking through his notes. "You've got some wood rot on the porches and a small leak in the roof, but the rest is just deferred maintenance and cosmetic stuff. It's amazing, really, considering this place is over a hundred years old. They sure don't build them like this anymore."

"Really? Over a hundred years old?" she asked. "I had no idea."

"Yeah," Gabe said. "I would guess it was built in the early 1900s, probably from trees on this property. Finn told me it was the first cabin in the Oasis, though it wasn't called that back then. This area has quite a history though I've never really looked into it. When I was a kid, I remember the old timers saying that a pioneer family settled this land. Maybe they built this cabin, but I can't say for sure. You might be able to find out more at the county courthouse."

"Wow, that is fascinating. Maybe I'll start digging into it and see what I can find. Maybe Finn knows more; I'll ask him. Speaking of Finn," she said," what an interesting man. What can you tell me about him?"

"Finn?" Gabe chuckled." How much time do you have?" She saw his eyes flash with amusement. "He's a character for sure and a local legend. He lives almost entirely off the land though I'm sure he doesn't have to. He just likes it that way. I've heard some pretty colorful stories about his past, but I'm not sure what is true. Rumor has it he was an Olympic boxing champion, but if you ask him about that, he just chuckles. I've never seen anyone who can clean a catfish faster or field dress a deer better yet, he prides himself on being a gentleman farmer. He's a bit of a mystery but one hell of a nice guy."

"He's been very kind to me; everyone has," she said as she met his gaze. She paused for a moment." I appreciate all your work here. I baked you some brownies, but it doesn't seem enough to thank you. To be honest, I'm a little overwhelmed with the house. Getting the property cleaned up for me was a big leg up."

"Brownies? I'll mow your lawn for brownies anytime you want," he said with a laugh and a twinkle in his eye. "Seriously, though, it was no trouble at all. With my tractor and the bush hog, it only took a few minutes. I'd be happy to keep it up for you."

Kennedy felt the emotion well up and into a lump in her throat. She wasn't used to feeling the warmth of this level of human kindness. She knew her eyes were glassy with unreleased tears, so she turned away so he wouldn't see and crossed the room to gaze out the window.

"So can you do the work on the house?" she said softly. "I'd love to get started whenever you are available."

"I can get started right away," he said. "As luck would have it, I've just finished up a job and have some time before I start the next one. Ok to start tomorrow?"

"Oh, that would be amazing, thank you," she said without turning to face him. She needed another moment to compose herself, her emotions still a little raw. There was an awkward pause as they struggled to move on from the moment.

"Well," he said when she finally turned to him, "I'm going to head out and get some supplies so I can start early tomorrow." He started for the door and stopped. "Ok to start at eight? If that's too early, I can come a little later."

"No, no, eight is fine," she said. "Is there anything you need from me? A deposit or anything?"

Gabe turned back toward her with a smile. "Just the brownies."

The long drive to the county courthouse gave her time to think. Now that Gabe had piqued her interest in its past, she was hungry to know more. He told her she might find things out at the old courthouse where the county maintained historical records. Managed by one of the county's most senior citizens, Olivia Lafayette, Gabe was sure she could at least point her in the right direction.

She was curious about the history of her little cabin and how the Oasis had come to be, but she couldn't help her mind from wandering and wondering about the new friends she'd met. Finn was a treasure, and she was glad he had been the first one she had gotten to know. His warm Southern charm and delightful sense of humor were food for her wounded soul, something she desperately needed. She was surprised they had connected so strongly so quickly, being the unlikely pair they were. But now that they had, she felt like she had known him for years. One thing was for sure; she was looking forward to spending more time with her new friend and engaging in his colorful conversations. She hoped he had more history about her cabin and the Oasis to share with her.

The old courthouse was a study in early Florida architecture. Like many other Florida courthouses, it had a distinct Romanesque style with its graceful arched entry and high clock tower. Built in 1902, its red brick exterior still looked fresh, and the native cabbage palms that framed its entrance accentuated it's old Florida feel. As Kennedy climbed the steps, she felt excitement at what she might learn inside the old, historic building. When she passed through its front doors, the sights and smells of the place told her it had a rich and colorful history. She felt like she had stepped back in time as she took it all in.

There was no security checkpoint in the huge vestibule area, a welcome change from the harsh realities of crime-ridden Miami. As she approached the man behind the receiving desk, she appreciated the absence of plexiglass barriers and bulletproof windows.

"Hi there," she said with a smile, "I'm looking for the historical records office. Can you tell me where I can find it?"

"Well," he said, as he pointed down the hall, "it's down at the end there, on the right, but I'm afraid it's not open right now."

"Oh," she said, clearly disappointed. She glanced at her watch. "Is it closed for lunch? Should I come back later?"

"No, I'm afraid it's closed for a few weeks. Miss Olivia, our volunteer, has gone to Waycross to visit her family. We don't expect her back until the end of the month."

"The end of the month?" Kennedy asked. "Is there anyone else who could possibly help me?"

"I'm afraid not," he said with a frown. "Miss Olivia runs that place, and she's got her own ways of doing things. She'd skin us alive if any of us started messing around in there. When the old bird passes on it's probably gonna take us years to figure it all out."

"Don't worry, Frank, she's probably gonna outlive us all," added a voice from one of the offices. Frank chuckled and nodded, and Kennedy smiled.

"Oh, well, I was trying to get some information on an old property I just bought," she said with a sigh." I guess it will have to wait. Thanks for your help." She turned to go.

"Come on back in when she gets back," Frank said. "If anybody can help you with that, it's Miss Olivia. There hasn't been a thing that's happened in this county for the last century or so that she doesn't know about."

"I will," she said as she waved over her shoulder. "Thanks again."

————————

The hammering coming from the porch was loud. So loud that Kennedy didn't hear the knock at her back door. It startled her when she finally heard a woman's voice calling out. She turned to see a woman she had never seen before standing at her back door. Even though she was a stranger, Kennedy saw she had a friendly face.

"Hi!" the woman said. "I'm Adsila Catawnee. I live just down the way. I just wanted to stop by and introduce myself and welcome you to the neighborhood."

"Oh, thank you," Kennedy said," I'm Kennedy, Kennedy Klark."

The two women shook hands, and Adsila placed her other hand over Kennedy's in a gentle, more personal gesture. The two women looked at each other for a long moment.

"You have quite the home here. Are you going to be living here full-time, or is this going to be a summer place?" Adsila asked.

37

"Oh, definitely full-time," Kennedy answered. " I've only been here a short time, and already I never want to leave!"

"Our Oasis tends to affect folks that way; it's a special place for sure. Is it just you or…" she said as she peered around inside.

"Yes, it's just me. I, ah, don't really, ah, have any family," she blurted out, then quickly changed the subject. "I'm sorry, would you like to come in for a cup of coffee or a glass of iced tea? I'm still getting settled, so it's a bit of a mess, but please come in," Kennedy stepped back and opened the door wider.

"Thank you, but I can only stay for a bit. I'm on my way to town." She stepped through the door, took a few steps, stopped, and looked around. "It's quite lovely, isn't it? It's got a very nice feel about it. A spiritual feel, actually. Do you feel it too?" Adsila asked as she turned toward Kennedy.

"Uh, yes, I do…um, I have, since I've been here," Kennedy stammered as she gestured to the oversized chair by the fireplace. "Please, have a seat. What can I get you?"

"Just a small glass of tea, please, that would suit me just fine," she said as she continued to look around. "I see our Gabriel is helping you get the place in shape. That was a wise choice; he will have you fixed up in no time."

"Oh, yes, I'm so glad he could start immediately. Finn says he does good work, and it's a relief to have someone helping me. Do you know Finn?" she asked, trying to keep the conversation light.

Adsila gave a hearty laugh. "Oh, honey, everyone knows Finn."

Kennedy laughed. "So Gabe tells me. He's quite interesting, and he's been so kind to me. We met in town at the hardware store, and he spent almost an hour helping me shop."

"Sounds like Finn," she said with a chuckle." He has a knack for showing up just where he's needed."

"How long have you lived here in the Oasis?" Kennedy asked as she handed her the tea.

"A long time, my mother brought me here as a young woman. I grew up as a child in the mountains of North Carolina. The first time I met Gabriel, he was a little boy. He used to come fish off our dock. His parents' place was on the high ground, but he always loved the river. They're gone now, but he still lives up there on the farm."

"Yes, I saw the farm, it's very beautiful. So, Gabe has lived here his whole life?" she asked.

"He has, except for when he went off into the service. He was gone for a few years but returned home after. He has a sister, but she left for college and never came back. She lives in Canada now, I think. I don't think they have seen each other in a long time."

"Oh," Kennedy said, the story tugging at her heartstrings a little. "Does he have a…Is he…?"

"Married? No, no, he's never been married. But don't you think some of the local gals haven't tried," she said with a wink." But he seems to be content living up there alone on the farm. It's a pity, really, he's such a fine man."

Kennedy's heart was suddenly sad for him as she remembered his kind, cornflower blue eyes. It seemed they were both lost souls, and she wondered if that was how he recognized the pain in her eyes. Maybe he had painful memories of his own. Perhaps he was running from the past too.

"Well, I better get going," Adsila said as she stood to go.

"Thank you so much for stopping by; meeting you was great. I appreciate you taking the time. I know so few people here," Kennedy said as they walked out onto the porch where Gabe was repairing some wood soffits.

"I've enjoyed meeting you too, Kennedy, very much," she said. "I hope to see you again soon." She turned to go, then turned back to face her. "Here in the Oasis, we gather on Sundays at our Pavilion to worship together. Do you know where that is?" Kennedy only nodded. "Perhaps you could join us this Sunday. You could meet some of the other folks here."

Kennedy was lost for words. She didn't want to offend Adsila, she'd been so kind to her, but she'd had no God in her life for many years. If any remnants of faith remained in her heart, they had been destroyed by what had happened in her recent past.

" Ah...I don't think...I just can't," she stuttered as she struggled to express herself. "Thanks for inviting me, but it's just not for me." She felt so bad. She could see the disappointment in Adsila's eyes.

"Well, perhaps another time, then," Adsila said in a cheerful voice. "I'll be seeing you, Kennedy," she said with a wave over her shoulder as she headed toward her car.

Kennedy stared at the lane long after Adsila's car was out of sight, deep in thought and regret. When she turned to go back inside, she caught Gabe looking at her and their eyes locked. She hadn't realized he had overheard their conversation and flinched slightly in embarrassment. But surprisingly, the look in his eyes wasn't judgmental. Instead, she saw understanding and compassion there. His gaze seemed to say *I understand. I've been there too.*

Chapter Three

"A new command I give you: Love one another. As I have loved you, so you must love one another." John 13:34

vening descended upon the little river community, and Kennedy filled the old claw-foot tub she'd admired since she arrived. Gabe had lit the pilot of the old water heater for her, and she was eager to feel the warmth of the water on her skin. Later, she hoped to find a good book and settle into the big chair by the fireplace. As she soaked in the tub, her thoughts drifted to cooler weather when she could read by the firelight, but with the heat of the summer pressing ever nearer, she knew that would be a while.

After her bath, she wrapped herself in her terry cloth robe and knew she needed to wind down and get ready for bed. With a glass of wine in hand, she perused the low bookshelf under the windows in the living room. It was overflowing with books, most of which were old hardcover editions, with some paperbacks mixed in. The top shelf held a collection of magazines, newspaper articles, and knick-knacks. As she moved the books around, she noticed with dread that she had more dust to tackle.

There were hundreds of books, and being as tired as she was, she couldn't choose which one to read. She decided, instead, to explore some nooks and crannies of the old cabin. Her trip to the courthouse had piqued her curiosity, and she was eager to learn something new about the place.

She poked around the cabin, looking into spaces she had not yet explored. The beautiful old carved antique desk that sat under the window in her bedroom was something she had meant to get to since she arrived. She stood back and looked at it for the first time. It was large, and her instincts told her the desk was utilitarian and not just for show. When she ran her hand over its smooth, worn top, she felt a hint of nostalgia and intuition someone had written something important there. She realized that the desk was much like the one that sat in her mother's bedroom in the house where she grew up. Her mother, an avid writer, would sit for hours at that desk, though Kennedy never knew what she was writing about as a child. The picture in her mind's eye invited in a barrage of emotions that crowded her brain, and she sat down hard on the bed as the thoughts and memories flooded in.

The family home where Kennedy grew up was in the old historic, upscale south Florida town of Coral Gables. Nicknamed *The City Beautiful,* George Merrick developed it during the Florida land boom of the 1920s. It had a small but robust business district, and its picturesque "Miracle Mile" consisted of upscale shops, fine dining restaurants, and a five-star hotel. It was considered an affluent neighborhood seven miles west of Downtown Miami. Being close to downtown, it was a haven for successful businessmen and their families wishing to live away from the hustle and bustle of the city. With its own police force and strict zoning laws, it was an idyllic enclave with intricately manicured lawns, winding driveways, giant electric gates, and costly security systems and cameras. The streets bore romantic Mediterranean names like Riviera and Granada, and the picturesque city's architecture was almost entirely Mediterranean Revival style. There were no standard street signs, only unique concrete placards on the ground by which to navigate.

Anyone with prime social standing was also a member of its exclusive country club. Every Sunday, Kennedy and her family enjoyed eating brunch there after mass at the domed Catholic Church of The Little Flower. The exquisitely beautiful church was built somewhat later than the city's founding and in a similar Spanish Renaissance style. Her parents had been married there years before.

Alongside the city's development was the University of Miami, constructed on 240 acres of land just west of US-1. There, Kennedy opted to obtain her undergraduate degree in Art History and her law degree, even though she would have had her choice of any Ivy League school after graduating Valedictorian of the local private Preparatory School. Her father had attended Harvard, as had her brother, and he had made it clear on more than one occasion that his disappointment in her choice of schools and area of study ran deep. He felt her undergraduate degree was "worthless," and her law degree, specializing in International Law, had been a waste of her talent and not what he had expected of her. She knew in her heart that at the center of his disapproval was his disappointment she had not followed in his footsteps and entered the family practice he had built. It had been his dream for her since she was a little girl.

As for her mother, she knew she had never been her favorite. That was probably an understatement if she was honest with herself. Her mother appeared devoid of motherly instincts for her. Instead, she seemed to save all the love and praise for her brother, Liam. As long as Kennedy could remember, her mother's rigid Catholic upbringing had been reflected in her parenting style with Kennedy but not necessarily with Liam.

Mary Theresa O'Brien Klark, in her youth, had attended an exclusive and strict all-girls Catholic boarding school. As an only child of a wealthy Connecticut banking family, she had been raised primarily by nannies and then by the nuns at Sacred Heart Academy in Palm Beach. While her parents traveled the world sailing in the summers and spending time at their vacation homes, Mary Theresa suffered at the hands of the austere and mostly cruel nuns.

During the summers, Mary Theresa had to fend for herself. While she had her home to return to, her parents were never there, only staff. She survived the summers by vacationing with her friends and their families, constantly feeling awkward and out of place. One summer, she was invited to Costa Rica by a school friend. The girls spent a glorious summer roaming the land and riding horses on her family's huge coffee plantation. Away from the cruelty of the nuns and the lonely home of her parents, it was the happiest time of her life.

While Kennedy's mother had never physically abused her, the emotional wounds inflicted by her had been heartbreaking. Her cold and critical nature set a cloud over everything Kennedy did. One would have thought that after everything she had been through as a child, she would have wanted to embrace a loving family. But it seemed her childhood experiences had left her void of the desire. She viewed children only as a burden.

Kennedy believed that was why Liam was her favorite. Liam required little attention, being content to do his own thing, even as a small child. Kennedy had a keen curiosity and inquisitiveness, which required answers and effort in rearing. Mary Theresa wasn't interested.

Her relationship with her father, Keegan Klark, was much easier, especially when she was a young girl. She was the apple of her father's eye and enjoyed his full attention when he wasn't at work. He was intrigued by her bright and curious mind and recognized himself in her appearance and personality. To her, he could fill in the gaps of her mother's indifference, even though he worked long and relentless hours. She often wondered how he filled in his own gaps though she had a few ideas about that.

Her father was tall, handsome, and an imposing figure, and he had a knack for taking over a room with his charm and wit. From him, she and her brother Liam got their distinctive black Irish features. He was a brilliant lawyer with the same inquisitive mind he had passed on to Kennedy, and he was fascinated with discovering how things worked. With his analytical mind and critical thinking skills, he always seemed to be the smartest man in the room.

He was patient with Kennedy and interested in her hobbies, sports, and academic pursuits. She had a few fond memories of finding him in the stands at her lacrosse games, knowing he'd had to move mountains to clear his schedule. He was slightly eccentric and had a creative side, tapping into it especially when he was creating unique arguments in the law. He was highly successful and a prominent attorney specializing in white-collar criminal defense, which had proven to be lucrative in a corrupt city like Miami. He was nothing if not a workaholic.

Her father seemed to keep the family stitched together. He planned elaborate and exciting family vacations that Kennedy had enjoyed and learned much from as a kid. With her mother detached and Liam usually doing his own thing, these were the times she had her father all to herself. And though his adventurous spirit took them all over the world, the time spent sport fishing in their own backyard, the Florida Keys, seemed to make him the happiest.

 Her father's love of boating and deep-sea fishing was one of the few things he shared with his son. They spent most weekends on the water, often in Biscayne Bay. He was meticulous about everything, but nothing compared to the time and attention he put into his boats. While not as passionate as his father about fishing, Liam enjoyed the boating life. Miami's water culture and their wealth gave Liam a steady stream of female companions. He had been in trouble with his father more than once for entertaining ladies in his parents' master stateroom.

Liam was genuinely brilliant and excelled at everything he did. He was handsome, having gotten, like Kennedy, the best of both of his parents' features. Like his sister, his almost black hair and blue-green eyes made him extraordinarily attractive, and his larger-than-life and charismatic personality made him magnetic to men and women. The men wanted to feed off his incredible energy. The women just wanted him.

He did everything better, bigger, and faster, whether in sports, academics, or socially. He earned all A's in his academic career, including Harvard Law. To his parents, especially his mother, he was perfect. To the world, he was perfect. But Kennedy knew better.

While her brother gained favor with her father by following in his footsteps, Kennedy knew he was a true opportunist at the heart of the matter. Liam was much like his mother, materialistic and shallow, and would do whatever was necessary to get what he wanted. While his father was proud of his son's accomplishments and for his picking up and carrying the family mantle, Kennedy knew in her heart it was not out of sentiment that Liam had done this. It was in his own self-interest.

Kennedy wanted to make it on her own. She didn't want to live in her father's or brother's shadow. While she successfully fought off the feelings of inadequacy and shame, it was difficult. Liam let no one forget how much better he thought he was, and her mother never let her forget that she felt Kennedy didn't measure up to him. She was sure she would have never made it through if it had not been for her father's love and attention. She had held her own.

As Kennedy pulled herself out of the haze, she realized she was still staring at the desk. While it was the catalyst, she knew the memories had been waiting for their release. She'd felt them bubbling under her consciousness for some time.

She felt profound sadness but an odd sense of relief at the same time. Remembering in excruciating detail had been therapeutic. She'd suppressed the memories for a while, afraid of the release and what may come with it. But now that she had let them out, she felt an unexpected and unrecognizable emotion. She wasn't sure what it was, but it was different. She took a long time to fall asleep as she wrestled with it, and when she looked at the clock for the last time, it was midway to morning.

When she heard the rattling on the front porch, it startled her. Looking at the clock, she realized she had slept past nine o'clock for the first time in a while. She could see Gabe's shadowy form moving around on the porch through the gauzy curtains on her bedroom windows. She guessed the rattling had been him moving his aluminum ladder around as he repaired the old porch's roof.

She swung her feet off the bed and planted them on the old heart of pine wood floor. She felt groggy and needed coffee, and she was worried she had missed her opportunity to share some with Gabe by oversleeping. Over the last few mornings, she had enjoyed watching him work, a cup in his hand while carrying on an interesting conversation with her. She slid into her jeans and wrestled on a t-shirt as she headed to the kitchen to put on a pot.

She cracked open the front door and peeked outside. Gabe was down at the far end of the porch, pulling down some old rotted wood.

"Sorry I'm late," she said, "do you still want coffee?"

"I thought you were never going to get up," he said without turning around.

She laughed. "I was up late and slept in," she said as she walked toward him." Looks like you are almost finished with the work on this porch."

"Mostly, though, there's a little more work here in this corner than I bargained for. But it's nothing that isn't fixable," he said, hands on his hips, staring up at the underside of the porch roof.

47

"What's keeping you up at night, Kennedy?" he said as he finally turned to look at her.

She felt a jolt of emotion at his directness but softened as his cornflower blue eyes found hers. "Nothing really," she lied. " I was just working on organizing the cabin and lost track of time."

He seemed to accept this answer as he circled his ladder, trying to get a better view of the rafters of the old porch.

"I need to head into town a little later to pick up some supplies," he said. "You feel like getting lunch? There's a great place I'd like to take you to. I think you will like it."

Kennedy was surprised at the invitation, but she took it at face value. They were friends, there was no reason to read anything else into it.

"Sure," she said. "Sounds like fun."

———————

When Gabe turned his pick-up off the main road and started down the bumpy dirt road, she had doubts. She looked at him inquisitively, but he didn't take his eyes off the road. He hadn't given her any details about where they were going, so she decided to go with it. She would discover what he had planned for her soon enough.

They came upon a small, one-story building with a low-slung roof line. It was old, Kennedy could tell, but quintessential old Florida. There was an "open" sign flashing in one of the windows, and when they cleared the trees and pulled into the dirt parking lot, she could see it resided on a pretty spot on the river.

"What is this place?" she said as she sat up a little straighter in her seat and peered over the dashboard.

"Miller's Fish Camp," he said without further explanation.

"Oh," she said, surprised. "Are we eating here?"

"Only the best for you, Kennedy," he said with a wry smile. "There are some picnic tables down by the water. Go find one in the shade, and I'll be down there in a minute."

While he was gone, she got a better look at the place. The property was beautiful, peppered with live oaks and some cypress trees down by the river. There was a small boat ramp with a wooden finger dock that ran alongside it. The building itself looked more inviting from the front. It had a large front porch that offered pretty views of the river, and she could see a beer sign in the window. She listened as the cicadas and crickets buzzed and chirped, but otherwise, it was quiet. As she gazed out at the river's clear waters, she saw a mullet jump twice, and the sounds of its splashing made her smile.

After a few minutes, she saw Gabe coming down the front steps. He had two white to-go containers stacked on top of each other in his left hand and two bottles of beer in his right. As he made his way down the sloping lawn to the shadiness of the river, she felt a twinge of attraction to him, but she quickly snuffed it out. She knew it was not the right time in her life to be getting involved with anyone.

He set the boxes and the beers down on the table, then wrestled his large frame into the picnic table, having to swing his long legs in from the side. He passed her a beer but not before he twisted the cap off for her and then opened his own. He lifted his beer toward her and then took a long swig. She followed along with him. The ice-cold beer was refreshing and went down easily.

"Well, dig in," he said as he passed out the containers. Kennedy opened her container, and the sight and smell of the food made her mouth water. There were two fried catfish filets on top of a mountain of fries with a couple of hush puppies tucked into the side. She broke off a small piece of fish and popped it in her mouth, chewing slowly and savoring its tender flavor.

"Wow," she said, "this is delicious." Gabe smiled and murmured as he chewed his food.

"So tell me about this place; it looks old." She waited while he finished a bite and washed it down with a sip of his beer.

"It is," he said." I used to come here with my dad a lot as a kid. We would launch our boat here to fish the river. They sell bait and tackle and ice, that sort of thing. They've got a small kitchen and a bar up front. It may look quiet now, but you should see this place on Friday and Saturday night," he said with a laugh.

"Really?" she said. She couldn't imagine it looking at the peacefulness of the place now.

"Yeah," he said with a laugh. "It's sort of the local watering hole. Finn hangs out here."

"What?" she said with amusement," Finn?" That was unexpected.

"Don't let the old codger fool you," Gabe said." He may be up in age a bit, but he's got a lot of vigor left in him. Rumor has it he's got a woman he sees a few towns over. He disappears for a few days every now and then, but nobody knows where he goes."

Kennedy laughed. "Well, good for him. I hope it's true. Everyone needs somebody to love."

She paused. She hadn't expected that to come out of her mouth. Gabe paused too, and they looked at each other for a moment. She shifted in her seat and changed the subject.

"So tell me more about this place. What's its history?" she asked.

"Well, old man Miller bought the place in the '40s, I believe, and built the building and put in the boat ramp. He ran it until he passed away a few years ago. His wife died young, and he only had two kids. His son never took much interest in the place; he lives up in Tennessee now, I think. His daughter and granddaughter run it now. She's a widow. Her husband took his own life a few years ago."

"Oh, how sad," Kennedy said, her voice soft as she gazed at the river.

"Yeah," he said quietly, "he was a veteran, couldn't hack the memories."

Kennedy noticed something in his voice change as though he knew more than he was saying, but he said nothing further. They were quiet for a minute, finishing their meal. Finally, he closed his container, pushed it away, and smiled at her.

"So," he said, "the repairs are mostly finished on the outside of the house. Are you happy so far?"

"Oh, yes," she said, beaming. "I never thought it would come together so fast. I'm still working on getting all the dust cleaned up inside, but it's starting to feel rather homey. Thanks for lighting the pilot on the water heater. Last night I got my first warm bath since I've been here," she said as she laughed.

Gabe smiled, "Well, you're welcome, and I'm glad you brought that up. I think you should probably replace that old thing sooner than later. It's ancient, and I'm kind of surprised it even fired up at all. Those old heaters tend to burst when they get long in the tooth. We don't need you coming home to a flooded house."

The thought horrified her. "Oh, is that something you can do, or do I need to hire someone else to do it?" she asked.

51

"I can do it for you. If you want, we can pick up a new one in town at the hardware store, and I can get it in this afternoon."

She sighed with relief. "That would be great; I had no idea I was living so dangerously," she said with a smile.

"I guess we better get going, then," he said as he untangled his large form from the picnic table. "Sometimes replacing these old things can get dicey. I wouldn't want to leave you with no hot water tonight."

———————

The clattering and clamoring from the utility room off the back porch were significant. Gabe had been right; removing the old beast was a difficult task. After a while, he emerged sweaty and irritated.

"Listen," he said," I know this isn't what you want to hear, but I'm not comfortable hooking up to that old wiring. I should have looked at it before we left for lunch." He glanced at his watch. "I can't get back to the hardware store before they close, and I don't have what I need up at my shop. I'm afraid I'm going to have to finish this up in the morning. I'm sorry. It's my fault, really."

"Oh," she said, a little disappointed that she wouldn't be able to enjoy a bath in her tub that night. "It's ok."

He could see the disappointment in her eyes and felt terrible about it. "Listen," he said. "I've got a little guest house up on my property. You're welcome to use it if you want a hot shower tonight."

"Oh no," she said with a smile. "It's fine, really, but thank you. I've sort of gotten used to cold showers. I'll survive until tomorrow."

"Ok then, I think I'm going to head out; there's not much more I can do here today. I'll see you in the morning, probably around nine. The hardware store opens at eight," he said as she followed him out to the porch.

As she watched him go, she felt that twinge of attraction again. She called after him. "Gabe? Thanks for lunch. Thanks for everything, really."

He paused for a second but then waved over his shoulder. Leaning against the post on the old porch, she watched him drive off in a cloud of dust and felt a little sad. She realized that, for the first time in a long time, she didn't want to be alone.

Chapter Four

"Two are better than one because they have a good return for their labor: If either of them falls down, one can help the other up. But pity anyone who falls and has no one to help them up." Ecclesiastes 4:9-10

Gabe fired up the old farm truck and headed to the pasture to feed the horses and goats and check on the cows. It was barely light out, and a velvety fog blanketed the farm, characteristic of cool North Florida mornings in the spring. As the day heated up, the mist would burn off, and by mid-morning, it would be gone. These early mornings on the farm brought him the most peace. He enjoyed the quietness and the contentment in the eyes of the horses and other livestock. It was when he felt that everything was working in perfect order.

As he leaned against the board fence, Belle, the old mare, came in to nuzzle him. She was getting on in age, but she was still his favorite. He fished an apple out of his pocket and offered it to her, and she eagerly nibbled at it. It was their morning routine, and as the other horses noticed and gathered around, he emptied his pockets of the carrots and apples he had brought them. He gave Belle a pet on the nose, glanced at his watch, and headed for the truck. It was barely seven, but he needed to be at the hardware store at eight o'clock sharp. It would be a hot day, and he wanted to install Kennedy's water heater before her utility room heated up like a sauna.

As much as he'd tried, he couldn't get the blue-green-eyed girl off his mind. They had gotten to know each other over the last couple of weeks, and he realized he had been taking his time getting the work done, knowing he wouldn't see her every day once he was finished. Aside from her natural beauty, something about her pulled at his insides and made him want to fix the haunting sadness he saw in her eyes now and then. When the sadness wasn't there, he admired her quick wit and obvious intelligence, but her vulnerability stirred up his protective nature. It had tugged at him since they had met on the road for the first time.

When Finn had brought her to him, he felt it was an incredible stroke of good fortune. He would have found a way to see her again but having this time with her was unexpected. As the days went by, he searched for ways to keep the connection going after the work at the house was finished. Lunch had been a delightful distraction, and he liked her easy-going nature and go-with-the-flow demeanor. While she was a girl raised in the sophistication of the city, he sensed that she had taken to the pace of rural North Florida. It was a relief to him it seemed she might want to stay there.

He gobbled down an egg sandwich and grabbed a piece of fruit as he went out the door. The sun was up in the sky now, and the cicadas had started their choruses. He passed the driveway to Kennedy's cabin and tried to find an excuse to stop in but couldn't. He needed to get to the hardware store anyway.

It had been a long time since a woman had gotten his attention. When he was younger, he had sown plenty of wild oats and smiled to himself as he remembered them. Things had been so simple then, and he'd had the self-confidence of a lion. He'd had his share of female escapades in his youth, but as the crush of real life had come, he'd found meaningless relationships less and less appealing. Things were complicated now. He was complicated now.

It was the complicated part that held him back. There was never a shortage of women who wanted his attention but he knew that once they got past the newness, the cracks would show, and the questions would come. When he had come home from the service, back to the farm and the river, he'd hoped things would go back to normal for him, but they never had. The memories of the things he'd seen and done in the cruelty of war would not release him. The nights were the hardest. Though he could keep the wolves away from the door in his waking hours, the dreams always let them in.

From a young boy, he had always wanted to be a Navy Seal. His dad had insisted he attend college first, hoping that the four-year distraction would cause him to lose interest. But, as soon as he graduated from the university, he went to see a Navy recruiter and began the long and brutal path to becoming a Seal.

When he returned home from his time in the service, it had not been easy. His mother had been diagnosed with cancer a few months before and was declining rapidly. His father, ten years her senior, was struggling to take care of her and the farm. Gabe moved back to the farm to help out, though he was struggling with his own demons, the after-effects of the missions and clandestine wars still fresh and raw.

His mother died on a glorious Sunday morning with Gabe at her bedside. His father, who had spent months caring for her, had taken a brief time away in the downstairs bedroom to rest. He would never forgive himself for not being there with her at the moment of her death and died a few months later of what, Gabe was sure, was a broken heart. Suddenly, Gabe was alone at a time when he needed his family the most. His sister never even came home for the funerals.

When Gabe contacted his sister about what they should do about the farm, she told him she was not interested in it. She and her husband were moving to Canada with their family, as he had been named the President of a large oil and gas company there. Gabe knew Sara Lee had not been home for many years, so the news didn't surprise him. When he told her he wanted to keep it, she said she would have her attorney contact him about the disposition of her half of the estate. He had expected to receive a buy-out proposition but was surprised to learn from the attorney she had relinquished her interest in the estate's assets to him. Apparently, she was cutting all remaining ties to North Florida, including him.

He and his sister had never been close. She was older as his mother had struggled to conceive. After his sister was born, his mother gave up on trying to have more children. Fourteen years later, Gabe came along during the change of life. He was raised like an only child, more like a grandchild to his older parents. His sister took no interest in him, and by the time he was old enough to remember her, she had left for college. He only saw her a handful of times after that.

He never understood his sister's disdain for her upbringing and lack of interest in a relationship with him. His parents had been loving, supportive, and kind, and the farm and the little river community had been an idyllic place to grow up. Gabe had learned to fish and hunt from a young age and spent many nights camping along the river with his dad. When he was around ten years old, his dad let him go on his own or with friends, as he was getting older and had less energy to devote to the boy. By thirteen or fourteen, Gabe had explored every nook and cranny of the woods along the river, could launch and run a boat expertly, and was an accomplished hunter and fisherman. He was also a good rancher, having learned to care for the animals at his father's side. Every morning before school, he had ridden with his dad, in the old farm truck, out to the pastures to help feed and water the animals. They were times he cherished, especially after his dad passed.

When he adjusted to living alone in the big old farmhouse and felt the farm was under control, he looked for a job. He didn't need the money; it was more a way to distract himself from the pain of loss and the memories. When he'd mentioned to one of his childhood buddies, the local sheriff, that he was looking for something, he was deputized into the department soon after. While it was a good fit for his background and skills, it was difficult. The mechanics of the job hit too close to home for him. He had been called out to a home in the far end of the county one night, late, due to a domestic situation. At the sound of a woman screaming and children crying, Gabe and his partner broke through the door. They found the woman bleeding on the floor, the children huddled and crying in the corner, and a man wielding a knife. When the man had come at Gabe, he had taken him down with one shot. He'd resigned the following day.

His dad had been a jack of all trades who could build or fix anything. Gabe had spent most summers building and repairing structures around the farm with his father and had become a skilled carpenter. He'd decided to get his contractor's license, buy a sawmill and do his own thing. It would occupy his hands and his mind and help keep the demons at bay.

It took the better part of the morning to replace the wiring and install the new water heater. He worked through lunch to finish the repairs on the back porch before the sun reached that side of the house. Though it was spring, working in the direct sun was miserable.

After their morning coffee, he had seen little of Kennedy, but he could hear her moving things around and cleaning inside the cabin. Occasionally, he would glimpse her through the screen door, but mostly she'd been out of sight. She'd set an insulated water cooler outside for him, for which he was thankful. Late in the afternoon, she came out and sat in a rocker with a glass of ice water.

"It's hot in there," she said, motioning over her shoulder and fanning herself.

58

"Those old window units probably can't keep up with this late afternoon heat. That's not going to get any better," he said, chuckling.

"I figured," she said and was quiet for a moment as he wrapped up his work. "What do you think I should do?"

"Well," he said," you could replace those units with newer ones, but I think you would be better off putting in mini splits."

"Mini splits?" she asked.

"Yes," he said. "I'm sure you've seen them. They are units that mount on the wall."

"Oh, yes, I know what you mean. I remember seeing those all over South America when I traveled down there. Is that something you can do?" she asked as she turned to look at him.

"I can. I just need to make some calculations, and I'll get the units ordered. Probably get them in next week. Will you make it till then?" he asked with a chuckle.

"I suppose." She laughed as she leaned back in her rocker, eyes closed, still fanning herself.

Gabe gazed at her. She looked beautiful in the late daylight, a thin bead of sweat on her brow and the pale skin on her graceful neck a rosy color from the heat. Her hair was pulled back from her face in a low knot accentuating her perfect facial structure of high cheekbones and a defined jaw.

"Want to cool off?" he asked, not taking his eyes off her.

"Cool off?" she said as she rolled her head toward him, her eyes fluttering.

"I'm going to run home and change, I'll be back in twenty minutes," he said as he walked to the truck. "Get your swimsuit on."

Kennedy sat in the front of the john boat as Gabe maneuvered it downriver. She hadn't seen the river this way yet, and she was awed by the beautiful scenery. The water was mostly clear with just a touch of the root beer color of the tannins from the cypress trees. She heard the call of the osprey and noticed him circling above, looking for his evening meal. She could see the mullet darting around ahead of the boat, and now and then, one would jump.

The sun was getting low in the sky, and the day's heat dissipated. There was a coolness in the air coming up off the water, and the river was tranquil except for a few bird calls and the sound of the boat motor.

After a while, Gabe navigated into a narrow run, and they had to duck around some overgrowth hanging out over the water. Soon the overgrowth disappeared, and the run opened up into a large spring, its crystal clear water a range of beautiful greens and blues. Gabe watched as Kennedy peered over the side of the boat in amazement at the clear water.

"Wow, this is beautiful," she said, her voice rich with emotion. "I've never seen anything like this."

Gabe smiled and was happy he had been the first to show her this magical place. "I've been coming here my whole life," he said. "It's the best swimming hole in the county." He pulled the boat over to a sandy beach, stepped out, and extended a hand to Kennedy. Gabe reached back into the boat when she was on sure feet and grabbed the small cooler he'd packed and two beach chairs. Kennedy stood at the water's edge, peering into the depths.

"How deep is it?" she asked.

"Down where the water boils out, it's about fifty feet. You going in?" he asked.

Kennedy didn't answer but waded in ankle-deep while Gabe got a couple of beers out of the cooler. She pulled her shirt over her head, tossed it onto the chair, and did the same with her shorts. To Gabe's surprise, she waded into the spring to her hips and then did a graceful dive. She emerged, wiping the water from her face.

"It's so cold!" she said laughing. "It took my breath away!"

"Yep," Gabe said. "It's always 72 degrees." He waded out and handed her a beer. "You know most people take it a little slower," he said with a smile. She smiled back at him and looked down at her feet.

"I can't get over how clear it is. Is it always like this?"

"It is most of the time. Sometimes if the river gets high, it will darken up some," he said. "You know there are hundreds of these springs all over this part of Florida."

"I've heard that, but I had never seen one until now. Are they all as beautiful as this one?" she asked.

"They are all beautiful, but they are all unique," he said. "I like this one because almost no one knows about it except locals. The land around this spring is privately owned, so you can only get here by boat. You would never find it if you didn't know it was here. As kids, we used to hike in here, but it's a good, long way. Some of the big springs that are open to the public get pretty crowded on the weekends, but there is never anyone here," he said as he looked around.

She looked at him and smiled, trying to imagine him swimming there as a little boy. She thought it must have been a wonderful childhood for him, growing up on the farm and spending the hot summer days on the river and in the springs. It was easy to imagine, looking at him now, standing shirtless, waist deep in the clear water. He still had a boyish look about his face with his fair hair and blue eyes. His frame, however, was anything but boyish. She had noticed his build through his t-shirts and jeans, but she had no idea how well defined his musculature was. She also saw a few scars on his midsection and thought to ask about them but held back. While they were getting to know each other better, it was too soon for that familiarity.

"Well, thank you so much for bringing me here," she said, smiling at him. "It's really like a private paradise."

He smiled back at her, happy she was as enthralled with the hidden spring as he was. This beautiful girl who had captured his attention continued to surprise him. While sophisticated and refined, she was not afraid to experience new and different things. He sensed a robust adventuresome spirit in her and longed to show her more of his world here at the river. Hopefully, in the coming days, he would get to spend more of this kind of time with her. He was grateful he might get the chance with more work to be done at the cabin.

With the day ending, neither wanted to leave the peaceful paradise of the spring. Kennedy sat in her beach chair, digging her toes into the sand and sipping her beer.

"Well," Gabe said," if we are going to get back before dark, we better get going." He stood and carried the cooler to the boat. When he turned around, she was still sitting in her chair, staring at the water. For a second, his heart sank, but when he looked at her eyes, he didn't see the haunting sadness there. Instead, he saw only peace and contentment, and for the first time in a long time, he didn't hear the distant barking of the wolves outside his door.

Finn was out in the yard when Kennedy pulled the Jeep down the driveway. When he saw her he waved his hat at her and gave her a big smile. She hadn't planned on visiting but had spotted a peach pie at the bake shop in town that made her think of him. Now she was looking forward to his cheery disposition that always put her in a good mood.

"Hello there, Kennedy!" he called as she walked up the drive. Kennedy just smiled and waved.

"I hope you like peach pie," she said, handing him the pastry in the white bakery box.

"Well, what's not to like about peach pie, darlin'?" he said with a broad smile. "Come on up to the house and sit with me a bit."

Kennedy followed him onto the front porch, where he offered her a seat on the little wicker couch. She noticed a vase of fresh wildflowers on the table by the door.

"Those flowers are pretty," she said. "Did you pick those around here?"

"Yep," he said. "Just down the lane there, on the right, there's a little patch blooming. I'm headed out tomorrow to see a friend, and I don't want to show up empty-handed. It's been a while since I've seen her." He gave her a wink and a smile, and Kennedy wondered if it was the woman Gabe had mentioned. "Which reminds me, Gabe and I are having dinner here at my place tonight. We've been trying to get together for a while to cook up some venison from a doe we took down during the season. Can you join us?"

"That sounds like fun," she said without hesitation. "I'll bring the wine."

Kennedy had never been inside Finn's little cabin, and she was surprised at its neatness and charming decor. He had an interesting and rather large collection of books on the beautifully built bookshelves on either side of the river rock fireplace, and as she perused the titles, wine glass in hand, she could hear Finn and Gabe talking and clattering away in the kitchen. She'd asked if she could help, but they had shooed her out of the kitchen with loud protests and much bravado, so she kept herself busy by taking in the interesting elements of Finn's living room. He had several hunting trophies on the wall up over the bookcases, including a gigantic buck, a monstrous boar head, and a mounted gator over the fireplace that looked to be about 12 feet long. The glass-top coffee table held a shadow box that interestingly displayed several exquisite Indian artifacts. At one end of the room sat an old, mahogany sideboard with carved claw feet repurposed into a bar and a round wooden table with four plantation-style chairs. An intricately carved writing desk sat under the window to the porch and held a magnificent, mounted pintail duck. Other beautifully mounted birds were on the walls around the room, all positioned as if flying in perfect formation. Covering the old oak floor was a rich, deep-gold Persian rug that accented the leather couch and overstuffed, upholstered chairs by the fireplace. The entire place was masculine but with a distinct sophistication, evidenced by the inlaid humidor on the mantle.

When she left Miami, she hadn't brought a lot, but she remembered a few special bottles of wine from her collection. When Finn asked her to join them for dinner, she picked a 2007 Napa Valley Schrader Cabernet Sauvignon to bring with her. It was a year that had produced spectacularly complex Cabernets, and she thought it would pair nicely with the gamey venison. When she presented the wine to Finn, she was surprised when he recognized it. He'd immediately opened it, decanted it, and set it on the table to breathe. The wine he'd poured for her was also delicious, and while she hadn't gotten to look at the bottle, she was sure it was also exceptional. It appeared Finn had a taste for the finer things in life.

After much fuss and a flurry of activity, Gabe called her to the table, where she saw an impressive spread of beautifully prepared food. Finn held her chair for her while Gabe retrieved the last of the platters from the kitchen, and finally, the three friends were seated. Finn held out his hands.

"Let's join hands," he said. Kennedy hesitated but would do nothing to offend Finn, so she took his hand first, then Gabe's. "Dear Lord, we thank You for gathering these friends together, both old and new," he said as he gave Kennedy's hand a slight squeeze, "and for this bountiful feast. And, Dear Lord, please don't let Gabe have overcooked the venison, Amen."

They all chuckled as Gabe passed around the platters of food, the smells making Kennedy's mouth water.

"This is wonderful," she murmured as she took a bite of the tender venison. "What's in this sauce?"

"That's Gabe's famous blackberry sauce," said Finn. "Tasty, isn't it?" Kennedy could only nod and smile. She had not had a hot meal like this in some time and had to pace herself, so she didn't overeat.

The three friends dined and swapped stories, though most were of Finn and Gabe's hunting adventures through the years. The delicious food, wine, candlelight, and interesting conversation set the stage for a memorable evening, and Kennedy felt warm and relaxed. She didn't want it to end.

Later, after they had finished the dishes and the evening was winding down, Kennedy turned to the two men. "Thank you both. I haven't had this much fun in a long time," she said, her eyes misting over.

"Likewise, darlin'," Finn said as he gave a bear hug and a kiss on the cheek. "Gabe, you gonna make sure she gets home, ok?"

Gabe nodded, and Kennedy protested. "Oh no, it's ok; I'm only just down the road!"

"Sorry, Kenny, we don't let our lady friends see themselves home around here," Finn said as he showed them to the door. Finn patted Gabe on the back and shut the door softly behind them.

"I'll follow you down and make sure you get in ok," Gabe said as he turned and headed to his truck. Kennedy could tell by the firmness in his voice there was no room for argument.

As she watched the lights of Gabe's truck in her rearview mirror, her heart pounded a little bit thinking about Gabe walking her to her door. They pulled down her driveway, and she got out ahead of him, hoping he would follow, but he only stopped, keeping his lights pointed toward her porch and back door. When Kennedy got to her door, she hesitated and turned to see if he might come, but she could see him sitting, stock still, behind the wheel. She gave him a wave and slipped inside, disappointment welling up inside her. She leaned against the door, resisting the urge to open it and run after him to invite him inside. *Get a hold of yourself,* she thought; *you are only friends.* But she knew, at that moment, that it was much more than that to her.

Chapter Five

"Now faith is confidence in what we hope for and assurance about what we do not see." Hebrews 11:1

By the time Kennedy made her way down to the river's edge the next morning, the mist was gone, and it had turned into a warm, sunny, beautiful North Florida day. The sky was pale blue and dotted with a few pillowy clouds. Kennedy walked along her riverfront beach and noticed the river was becoming clearer as the high water of the early spring months was receding and, in shallower parts, you could easily see to the bottom. She kicked off her flip-flops and stepped gingerly into the water. The river water, at 72 degrees year-round, felt good on her feet. Finn told her the waters were considered healing by some, a natural remedy for aches and pains that come with exertion or old age.

She decided she would talk to Gabe about building her a dock so she could better enjoy her riverfront. It would provide her a place to sit, watch the water, or even fish. The shoreline and beach were in their natural state. Beautiful, but not easily enjoyed with the overgrowth, cypress stumps, and lime rock sticking up through the sand.

She had asked Gabe about the riverfront, and he had agreed that improving the outdoor areas was a good idea and would make living on the river more enjoyable. She wondered how long he would put up with her finding him more things to do. She was sure he had other clients and orders he needed to attend to at the sawmill.

Near the shoreline's end was an old lean-to she hadn't explored. When she looked inside, she was surprised to find an old wooden canoe that, remarkably, was in near-perfect condition. She hadn't been canoeing since her summers away at camp in North Carolina, but she was intrigued by the thought of taking it out on the river. She dragged it out to the river's edge and used the river water and an old bucket to clear away the dust and the spider webs. She let it dry in the sun while she got a paddle from the shed and went to the house to grab some water and her cell phone. She was excited for her first real solo exploration of the river.

She pushed the canoe off the shore and paddled away from the eddy that swirled past the cabin as the river started the big s-turn in front of her cabin. From there, she crossed over the shallow shoal, missing the bottom and catching some speed from the current as the river bent back to the left. As the torrent from the fast waters settled around the bend, the river became quiet, and the view downriver ahead of her was serene. She saw deer drinking at the riverbank and the many turtles sunning themselves on the tangles of downed trees and overgrown branches. She noted the old high water marks on the giant cypress trees and was surprised to see just how high the river could get. She also kept a watchful eye out for gators. Though she was a Native Floridian and used to seeing them, she didn't want to encounter one unaware.

She wasn't planning on this being a long excursion. She thought she would paddle down to Adsila's dock and tie off there. Later, Gabe might help her get the canoe back up to the house. She was enjoying the sights and sounds of the river and hadn't noticed that the sky had turned dark until she heard the low rumbling of thunder in the distance. She then realized she hadn't checked the weather before she'd left.

Hoping to make it to Adsila's dock before the rain came, she picked up the pace and paddled in earnest, taking advantage of the downriver current. Around every bend, she looked anxiously ahead for Adsila's dock, but, not knowing the river, she had miscalculated the distance by not accounting for all its curves and turns. When the first drops fell, she felt a slight panic rise in her chest. The rain turned from a few huge drops to a pelting, stinging rain in a few minutes, so hard that she could barely see the river in front of her.

She quickly paddled the canoe to the bank, where there was a sandy area and a small spring trickling out of the riverbank, seeking shelter under some cypress trees. She was on the opposite side of the river from her cabin, which was in a different county.

As she got out of the canoe, it tipped and took on water in the back, causing her flip-flops and the paddle to float out and into the current. As she hurried out into the water to catch them, she stepped on one of the craggy rocks and felt a sharp pain on the sole of her left foot. When she got back onto the sand, she saw that her foot was bleeding, the blood from the wound soaking into the white sand where she walked. She was in trouble, and she knew it.

Gabe was working at the cabin, having arrived in the late morning after she'd left in the canoe. He'd had work on the farm that morning and an order at the sawmill he needed to finish. He was surprised that it didn't appear that Kennedy was home, even though her Jeep was behind the house. He'd looked for her and saw where she'd been down by the water, walking around and cleaning out the shed, but she was nowhere in sight. To say he was a little concerned was an understatement.

When his cell phone rang and her number appeared on the caller ID, he was relieved, but the relief was instantly gone at the sound of her voice. Her voice was cracking as she explained her predicament. He could tell she was shaking, probably from the cold, and she had to yell over the pounding rain for him to hear her. Gabe heard the panic in her voice and felt his own panic rise when he realized she was out on the river in a bad storm. After catching a few details, he thought he knew where she was and told her he would be there as quickly as he could. He would have to go by boat. Since she was on the other side of the river, it would be a good 30 to 40 minutes if he drove.

Gabe ran to the truck, jumped in, and drove as fast as he could to Adsila's dock, where he kept his pontoon boat. He quickly released it from its moorings and started upriver toward where he thought she would be. Even with the canopy top up, the rain was pelting and relentless. While he drove with one hand, he dropped the clear plastic sides down with the other. Once he got her, he would need to get her under cover and warmed up quickly. Even though it was a warm day, hypothermia was a real threat if she'd fallen in the water and was out in the rain.

He thought she must not have checked the weather, as the weather prediction was that the storms would roll in early and be tumultuous. He had to constrain himself not to be angry with her, realizing that she was unfamiliar with the river and how quickly the weather could change. He also realized how important she had become to him in a short time. The thought of her hurt and in trouble seemed unbearable to him.

His eyes darted up and down the shoreline as he pushed the pontoon boat to its upper limits of speed. When he saw her under the cypress trees, huddled down with her arms wrapped around her, he thought his heart would leap out of his chest. The hard rain was turning to hail by the time he pulled the boat up onto the small beach, and he was alarmed to see blood trickling down the white sand and into the river. He could see that she was holding back tears and shivering, so he quickly got her into the boat and inside the enclosure. He pulled dry towels out from under the seats, wrapped her up with one, and used the other to wrap up her foot. He pushed the pontoon off the bank, turned it around, and headed for shelter. They would have to leave the canoe and its contents there for now.

They didn't speak on the ride back to the cabin; the torrential rain pounding on the truck's cab would have made it impossible anyway. It gave Gabe a little time to calm down now that he knew she was safe and it didn't look like the cut on her foot was serious. At the cabin, he told her to get in a hot shower, stay there for at least ten minutes, and clean her foot as best as possible. His Navy Seal training had taught him about triage, and he was still concerned about hypothermia and wanted to be sure she got her wound rinsed well with fresh water before he treated it. After Kennedy was showered and in a warm pair of sweats, he sat her on the couch where he had a first aid kit on the coffee table.

"Let me see your foot," he said as he sat down and patted his lap. She hesitated out of embarrassment, but the look on his face told her there was no room for argument.

"I think it's ok," she said as she reluctantly placed her heel on his thigh. He said nothing as he craned his head to the side to get a better look.

"Well," he said. "I'm more concerned about infection at this point. There are some pretty nasty bacteria in that river water. It does look like you could use a couple of stitches, but it's a pretty ragged cut. I think we can clean it up and butterfly it closed."

"Ok," she said. "You sound like a doctor. Have you had medical training?" He glanced up at her and their eyes locked for a moment.

"Just a little in the Navy," he said as he worked on the wound. They were quiet while he worked, Kennedy watching his face and noticing the tenderness with which he was attending to her. She felt terrible putting him through all that and foolish for putting herself in such a dangerous position.

"I guess I don't need to tell you that it was a bad idea to take the canoe out by yourself today, especially without checking the weather," he said, finally, as he put the last piece of tape on her bandage.

"No," she said quietly, "you don't." She paused for a minute, not sure what to say. "Listen, Gabe, I'm really sorry, and honestly, I don't know what I would have done if you hadn't answered your phone. I-I really don't." She felt the emotion well up inside her chest as tears sprang to her eyes.

"It's ok," he said as he tenderly set her foot on the sofa. "It's all over now."

Gabe felt that familiar tug at his insides as he watched her struggle through her apology. He wanted to pull her to him, hold her close and tell her it was ok but he felt paralyzed by his emotions. She seemed so capable and independent, yet so vulnerable at the same time. Her expressive eyes were like windows into her embattled soul, and when he could see the pain there, raw and unvarnished, all he wanted in the world was to take it away. One day, he hoped he could.

Kennedy was waiting for him on the porch when he got to the cabin the next morning, her wounded foot propped up on a little footstool. He suspected she'd been there for a while by her posture and the empty coffee cup in her hand.

"Good morning," he said. "How's the foot?"

"Throbbing, thank you," she said in a tired voice.

"I'm sorry," he said with a frown, "did it keep you up all night?"

"No, not all night," she said, leaving it at that. "Coffee?" she said as she struggled to get to her feet.

"I can get it," he said quickly, relieved when he saw her settle back into her seat. He pointed to her foot. "I want to have a look at that this morning." She only nodded and turned her gaze back to the river.

When Gabe had his coffee in hand, he pulled another chair over in front of her where he could sit to examine her foot. After carefully unwrapping the bandage, he looked at it for a moment, then softly prodded around the wound. He saw her flinch and mumbled an apology.

"Well," he said. "It's not overly red-looking, and it's not hot to the touch, so I don't think there's any infection brewing." He fished a tube of antibiotic salve and a large band-aid out of his shirt pocket. After redressing the wound, he looked up at her, still holding on to her foot.

"Let's just keep an eye on it for the next couple of days, ok?" She nodded and smiled at him. The warmth of his hands on her foot made her feel good, and she was reluctant for the moment to end.

"Thank you, Gabe, you're very sweet to worry about me." Gabe smiled back at her but didn't reply. Instead, he got up and carefully placed her foot back on the footstool.

"I think you should sit right there with that foot elevated today and keep me company while I work out here. I noticed some wood rot around this window that I'm going to replace," he said without looking at her. She smiled. There was nothing in the world she would rather do.

They spent the morning talking while he worked. Her resident osprey visited and spent the morning eyeing her from his high perch in the cypress tree. She got up a few times to hobble inside, to get them some tea, and eventually to make lunch. Though her foot was sore, she could get around while walking on her heel to keep the pressure off. As the noon hour rolled around, she called him inside, and he was surprised to see a nicely set table of sandwiches and fruit and a couple of tall glasses of iced tea.

"Kennedy, you didn't have to do this. Walking on that foot can't feel good," he said with a frown.

"It's ok. I can manage to hobble around a bit." She laughed. "Besides, I thought you might want a break from the heat today, and I do owe you for rescuing me yesterday."

"You don't owe me," he said, giving her a look more serious than she expected. They were quiet as they ate, and after Gabe had finished his sandwich and taken a long sip of iced tea, he looked at her.

"Listen, if you think you can get that foot into a shoe by this weekend, I'd like to take you to see some of the more interesting parts of the river," he said.

"Oh," Kennedy said. "I would love that!"

"Good, then let's plan on getting out early Saturday morning. I can pick you up out front on the pontoon boat, and we'll go see some of the river. Besides," he said with a wink and a smile, "I need to do something to keep you from wandering off by yourself."

For the next few days, they saw little of each other. With a slight lull in the work at the cabin before the air conditioning equipment arrived and starting the dock, Gabe could do some things at the farm and for other clients. He had been pushing work off for a while to spend more time at the cabin and with Kennedy.

Now he needed to take care of things to clear the way for the work she had planned for him.

Kennedy, without the distraction of Gabe at the cabin, turned her attention to better organizing some of the rooms now that she had completed the bulk of the cleaning. She'd spent more time in the kitchen, organizing the existing cookware and figuring out what else she might need to make it functional. Since she was not much of a cook, she was perplexed by some of the old-fashioned gadgets she found, but she held onto them, reluctant to part with anything.

She'd also been trying to devise a plan to update the kitchen's look without compromising its rustic roots. Gabe had suggested some fresh paint on the cabinets, refinishing the old butcher block countertops, and new lighting. He had also suggested adding a work island to the center since the kitchen was big. He felt he could match the original style of the cabinets and purchase a butcher block slab for the top. She couldn't have been happier with his suggestions.

Kennedy focused on the antiques in the living room, carefully cleaning and restoring their luster. She had beautiful pieces and formulated a plan to work them into a design that would include both the old and the new. She also tackled the bookcase, cleaning the old volumes and categorizing them on the shelves. Though it was painstaking work, at least she could sit on the floor and rest her foot while getting something important done. Most of all, she looked forward to Saturday and their outing on the river together.

Saturday, at dawn, Kennedy hobbled down the lawn to where Gabe was waiting on the pontoon boat. He extended his hand, first taking her bag, then hoisting her onto the front. He motioned her to the back, where she sat across from his captain's chair behind the helm as he backed the pontoon boat off the bank.

The morning was cool, and she was thankful for the light jacket she had put on at the last minute, especially as the pontoon boat got up to speed. After a few minutes, Gabe slowed to idle speed, pulling into a small eddy where the river made a long and graceful bend.

"I thought we would fish a little while they might be biting and have a little coffee. Does that suit you?" She smiled and nodded. She couldn't think of a more perfect way to start the day.

She sat while Gabe poured coffee from the thermos, noticing he had prepared it the way she liked it, sweet with half and half. He handed her a cup, poured himself one, and sat back in his chair, looking at her.

"Beautiful morning," he said. "Dawn and dusk are my favorite times of the day on the river."

"Mmm, I agree," she nodded, enjoying the sunrise colors and the quiet conversation. "I've seen a lot of beautiful sunrises in South Florida, but nothing that compares to the ones here on the river." Gabe felt his heart lift a little. When she said things like that, it gave him hope she would stay.

"You ready to fish a little?" he said as he reached for a rod and reel behind him. She nodded enthusiastically, and he handed it to her. "Just hold onto that for a minute," he said as he pulled a container of bait out of one of the holds." I'll bait that hook for you in just a minute."

"I can do it," she said as she opened the container, pulled out some bait, and walked to the front of the boat. He watched as she deftly baited the hook, flipped the bail, and made a perfect cast, landing it a few feet from the bank a good distance away.

"Girl," he said, "where'd you learn to cast like that?"

"I grew up fishing with my dad," she said as she started slowly reeling in the bait, not taking her eyes off her line. "Mostly saltwater, but we did some freshwater fishing as well. It was his first, great love." He saw her eyes mist over for a second, so he didn't pursue the subject. He sat and watched for a moment, wondering if this girl would ever stop surprising him. In the morning light, she could not have looked more beautiful; her perfect profile etched in gold as the morning sun's rays danced off the water behind her.

Then, as he reached for his pole, he saw her eyes widen and her face break into a huge grin as the line went taut with the pull of a fish and her rod bent toward the water. He grabbed the dip net and admired her skill as she expertly brought the fish up next to the boat where he could scoop it up.

"Wow, that's a pretty bass, Kennedy. Are you gonna out-fish me today?" he said, laughing.

"That was fun," she said, laughing with him. "It's been a while since I've done that." He heard the sentimentality in her voice, and to not stir up that sad look in her eyes, he didn't question her.

They watched as the unhooked bass slithered out of Gabe's hands back into the depths of the eddy. He could tell something about the moment stirred things up inside her. He hoped someday she would trust him enough to tell him what it was.

As the day warmed up and brightened, Gabe maneuvered the boat further upriver, pointing out some interesting sights along the way. In one part of the river, where it narrowed, some high rocky banks made it feel like they were passing through a canyon. They passed over and around several shoals as Gabe, with his knowledge of the river and skill with a boat, got them through places she felt would have discouraged even the best of boaters. At one point, he pulled the boat to the riverbank to show her where a natural siphon sucked in the river water. Then showed her where it was gushing out of a fissure at another place that sat back off the river a few hundred feet. As the day's heat set in, he pulled over into a small spring where they shared a picnic lunch and cooled off in the water.

The day flew by, and she did not want it to end. On the boat ride back to the Oasis, the sun setting quickly, Gabe said little. He looked lost in thought and seemed a little pensive though Kennedy couldn't imagine why. When they got to her house, he helped her bring her things in from the boat, and she thought to invite him in but worried she had taken up too much of his time. On impulse, though, she took a leap.

"Would you like to come in for a nightcap? I've got some cheese and crackers and fruit too if you're still hungry." Gabe hesitated, and her heart sank. He looked down, then out over the darkening river before he spoke. When she looked into his eyes, they were full of emotion.

"Thank you, Kennedy, but I can't tonight." She felt the disappointment wash over her like a tidal surge, and she suddenly felt foolish. "Listen, though," he said. "I'd really like you to come to the Pavilion in the morning. I think you would like it and you could meet some more of the people here in the Oasis. It's nothing formal. We just gather around ten o'clock."

"No," she said as she looked into his eyes, "I gave up on going to church long ago, Gabe. God has let me down too many times." There was an awkward pause as he sensed an edge in her voice. She sighed and looked away. "But, I appreciate the invitation, and thanks so much for today; it was really nice of you to take me out on the river."

Gabe felt a loss for words. He wanted to question her about her lost faith and the cynicism he had heard in her words, but something told him now was not the time. Instead, he gave it one last try.

"I think it would surprise you; it's not what you think. I don't mean to push; it's just that I thought it would be a good experience for you after the time we spent on the river today." He paused and looked at her face, trying to read her thoughts. "But I understand, maybe another time."

He turned to go, and she let him. The emotions overwhelmed her heart too much for her even to speak. She watched him as he went down to the river's edge, boarded the boat, and backed it away from the shore. He waved at her as he turned the boat downriver and disappeared into the darkness. Kennedy sat down in the rocker on the porch and felt the loneliest she had ever felt and wondered how that was even possible.

Chapter Six

"The Lord is close to the brokenhearted and saves those who are crushed in spirit." Psalm 34:18

A misty layer blanketed the Oasis, which was persistent even though it was approaching mid-morning. Gabe walked along the narrow lanes from the farm to the Pavilion as he did every Sunday morning. There was something about the walk and taking in the sounds of the birds and the sights of the wildlife that prepared his heart and his mind.

This morning, though, his mind was preoccupied with the blue-green-eyed girl. It had been excruciating to leave the evening before, knowing he had hurt her and probably left her angry. He should have accepted her invitation and stayed for a while, but he had been afraid, not of her but himself. He wasn't ready, and he was not whole. She deserved better. Still, the memory of the hurt in her eyes had left him sad and lonely. He so desperately wanted to be what she needed and wanted.

He'd invited her to the Pavilion as a bridge, perhaps a way for them to cross the deep crevasses of their wounded souls to get to one another. He had known she was damaged, even before she'd told him. He had recognized the haunting sadness in her eyes the first time he'd seen her. Now, he was angry with himself for letting her trust and letting her down. Even though it was unintentional, it felt cruel, nonetheless.

When he got to the Pavilion, everyone was gathering there, but the warm reception he got did little to soothe his troubled mind. He hoped he would feel better when the gathering was over, but he had doubts. Until he could see her again and try to fix what he had broken, he knew things wouldn't be right.

The old open-air tobacco barn looked beautiful in the morning mist, its rich, old, chocolate-colored wood in brilliant contrast to the bright green of the late spring landscape around it. Inside, the warm glow of the rustic overhead lighting lifted his mood. Even though it was an old barn, it held an unmistakable reverence. He found a seat mid-way back in the chairs set up every Sunday morning and admired the spray of fresh wildflowers that adorned the makeshift podium that served as a pulpit. Nothing about the Pavilion resembled a traditional church other than the old wooden cross that hung high on its back wall.

As the inhabitants of the Oasis filed in and took their seats, he noticed Adsila busying herself near the front, readying herself for the message she was to deliver this Sunday morning. Her eyes caught his, and she cocked her head as if to say *is she coming?* He reluctantly dropped his gaze and shook his head. He didn't want to see the disappointment in her eyes. He had hoped to deliver on the promise he had made to Adsila to persuade Kennedy to come.

Adsila slipped behind the podium as the little gathering fell silent. She smiled as she began her welcome and talked about the theme of her message. As she spoke, Gabe detected a slight pause as her eyes lifted to the back of the Pavilion, and her smile broadened. He glanced over his shoulder to see Kennedy standing at the wide entrance, wondering where she should sit. He raised his hand and motioned her over, realizing that he had picked a seat with an empty one beside it. She slipped in beside him, and they exchanged smiles, although hers was weak and full of discomfort and apprehension.

She sat upright and rigid in a formal posture he suspected was ingrained in her from many years of attending traditional religious

81

services. Instinctively, he put a hand on her back as a signal to relax, and she slumped a little and leaned his way. As Adsila began her message, it could not have been more poignant and personal. She talked about how God showed his perfection in everyday things. The beautiful sky, the moving river, the wildlife that grazed magnificently in the grass, in the kindness of those around us. We didn't have to look far to see His grace, only in our backyards. That finding God was easy; one only had to look beyond our earthly troubles to experience His love and salvation.

Gabe glanced at Kennedy and saw a tear slide down her cheek, her gaze straight ahead and trained on Adsila. He reached over, found her hand, and gently squeezed it. When she looked at him, her eyes said *I've missed this. I should have never let it go.*

They didn't talk about the Sunday at the Pavilion in the days that followed. Gabe was relieved, though, that the tension between them had dissipated, and he was optimistic that, perhaps, they could build something after his experience with her at the Pavilion. Things had been different between them, for sure.

Inspired by Finn's cabin and his eclectic style, Kennedy was contemplating how she might arrange the old antiques in her cabin when she heard a knock at the door. She turned to see Adsila standing in the doorway.

"Hello, the house!" Adsila called out." I'm headed to town. Can you join me, Kennedy?"

Kennedy's mood brightened at the sight of Adsila. "Yes," she answered. "I'd love to!"

The timing of Adsila's invitation was perfect. Kennedy had wanted to return to the small antique store on Main Street in the nearby historic town to reconsider a Persian rug she'd admired there. Adsila mentioned to her that there was also an interesting Art

Gallery in town owned by a woman, an artist herself, with artwork depicting the surrounding area. There was a good-sized artist colony there drawing from the local talent, which Kennedy found interesting for such a rural area.

As they chatted on the way into town, Kennedy studied Adsila's features. Her strong profile featured a sharp nose and chiseled cheekbones. Her skin was a natural, deep, rosy color that gave away her Native American roots and was the perfect complement to her almost black hair. Her build was sturdy but not slim. If you had a good enough imagination, you could picture her centuries ago as part of the tribe that was her heritage. She was also a good conversationalist, and the dialogue between her and Kennedy was light-hearted and effortless. Kennedy guessed Adsila's age to be in her early 50s, although she didn't look her age and had a genuine and youthful spirit.

"So you like our little community then? Do you think you will stay?" she asked. Kennedy was a little surprised at the question but guessed it was probably on the mind of all of her new friends. They all knew she was new to country life.

"I can't imagine living anywhere else now," Kennedy said, a little subdued. The question had stirred up some emotions hard to hide. She changed the subject. "You've been here a long time, Adsila; how does it compare to growing up in North Carolina?"

"In some ways, it's similar; in many ways, it is different," Adsila began, and Kennedy could tell by her voice she was sentimental about her childhood memories. "I grew up in the mountains of Western North Carolina in an area called the Qualla Boundary. My parents were descendants of the few hundred Cherokee who stayed when the rest of the tribe were removed and sent to Oklahoma - I'm sure you've heard of The Trail of Tears. Those who stayed gave up their Cherokee citizenship, assimilated, and, in exchange, became United States citizens. My mother, though a Christian, passed along much to my brother and me about our Cherokee culture and heritage. She even taught us the traditional language. Over time, the town of Cherokee became quite the tourist attraction and lost some of its appeal to my mother. After my father died, she brought us here to North Florida, ready for a change, I think. She passed away just a few years ago. My brother died not long after."

Kennedy was quiet for a moment as she sensed the sadness in Adsila as she told her about her life and family. Adsila took a deep breath and smiled.

"So you see, Kennedy, our little Oasis is a healing place. Broken hearts and souls are mended here," she said as she pulled into a parking space in front of the gallery. She put an arm around her and patted her shoulder as Kennedy bit back the tears. She wanted to tell Adsila she was alone in the world too but it was not the right time.

Kennedy realized the gallery was not far from the antique store, and she wasn't sure how she had missed it before, with its bold and colorful art in the storefront glass windows. Adsila introduced the owner, an older woman named Cadence Carr, who Kennedy found interesting. She studied the woman as she told them about some of the new works that had come in. She was bohemian in her appearance; her long gray hair and colorful, gauzy dress made her look worldly but earthy. She wore lots of jewelry, mixing metals and mediums, and Kennedy guessed she was well-traveled as she had a touch of an accent, though she couldn't place it.

Covering the gallery walls were paintings and photography and the display shelves had many pieces of local pottery and pieces of handmade jewelry. In the back, there was a small area in the store where they sold art supplies. All the artists were native to the area, and the artwork depicted scenes from the river or the surrounding landscape.

As luck would have it, Cadence had just set up a gallery show, an event she hosted twice a year. The show allowed local people interested in the art to meet the artists and the artists themselves to present and promote their works.

As Kennedy perused the paintings and photographs, she found herself drawn to the scenes of the native flora and fauna of one artist in particular. Wanting to take something home with her, she chose a small painting that depicted turtles sunning themselves on the downed trees in the river. It reminded her of the day on the river with Gabe, seeing them along the banks and sliding into the river as they passed by on the boat.

Later, at the antique store, Kennedy stood back to get a full view of the Persian rug she was thinking about for the cabin's living room. As she stood, arms crossed, considering it, Adsila came up next to her.

"That's beautiful, Kennedy, that would look wonderful in your living room," she said. "I think you should buy it."

"You think so?" she asked, her mind's eye still trying to picture it on the old heart of pine floor.

"I do," Adsila said. "And I'm sure we can get it into the car if we fold it in half." Kennedy noticed the rug was larger than she remembered but would still fit nicely in the room. It was gently used, in good condition, and the price was a bargain. More importantly, the colors were right, and the rug would give the room a rich but comfortable feel, something she was looking for after spending time in Finn's living room.

"Ok," she said, with excitement in her voice, "I think I'm going to get it."

After Adsila left for home, Kennedy retreated to her porch with a glass of wine to watch night fall upon the river. As she retraced the events of the day, she smiled. It had been nice to spend time with a female friend, something she had not done in a while. And it had been fun to add something to the cabin to make it more her own. While she still had quite a lot to do, she felt it was coming together nicely.

When she bought her condo on Brickell, she had turned the entire place over to a designer. Though the place was beautiful with its clean lines, monochrome creams, and grays, you couldn't call it warm. That suited her well; its minimalistic furnishings were the perfect environment for someone who was never home. Now, she craved the warmth and comfort the little cabin offered.

Who would have thought she would end up in a place like this, a world away from her fast-paced city life? She suspected the long work hours, the cool, impersonal condo, and her divergence from the career path expected of her were all a way to isolate herself from becoming too attached to anything. Now that she was finding true friendships and real connections, she felt sad, in some ways, for her former self. The sense of belonging she felt here was new to her but had some fears and risks of its own. With all her self-confidence as a high-powered woman in her former life, had she been a coward deep down? Had she used the sterile life she had created to insulate herself from the risks of feeling anything and therefore being hurt? The self-evaluation was painful. At that moment, she realized what she had given up and, sadly, that she could never get it all back.

Kennedy decided to tackle the extra bedroom since Gabe would be working inside all day starting the installation of the air conditioning. At least there, she could stay out of his way without having to sit out on the porch in the heat all day. She thought about going out somewhere but, honestly, couldn't think of where to go that would be enjoyable by herself. She could drive to the nearest city, but the thought of traffic and lots of people didn't appeal to her. And, if she were home, she could at least make him lunch and maybe get in a little conversation.

His rejection of her the other night had cut deep; if she were honest, its sting still lingered. The closeness they had shared on the river that day had not seemed to wane, but she still didn't understand why he had turned her down. Though the way he had put his hand on her back and squeezed her hand at the Pavilion on Sunday morning had felt intimate, she could still feel reluctance from him to get close to her. He seemed content with the way things were. She guessed she would have to be as well. In that realization, she had backed off just enough so he felt no pressure from her. If all they could ever be were friends, she didn't want to do anything that might risk that.

The extra bedroom needed little. Kennedy had bought new linens for the bed and some pretty towels for the small bathroom that adjoined it. The closet was mostly empty, with a couple of old boxes and a stack of magazines on the floor. Besides that, it needed a more thorough cleaning than the first pass she had given it when she'd gotten there.

She was washing the windows when she saw a red truck pull down her driveway. At first, she was confused, but then she quickly realized it was Finn coming to see her, or maybe Gabe. She had only seen him briefly at the Pavilion on Sunday and not otherwise since the dinner party. Her heart lifted at the sight of his fedora hat with its feather coming around the truck toward the door. The bedroom door was closed to block out the construction noise, so she could barely hear him and Gabe talking. When she distinctly heard her name, she wanted to see what was happening. She cracked the door open and found them standing in the living room, then opened it wide.

"Well, there she is!" Finn boomed." How are ya 'darlin'?" he asked as he crossed the room to give her a hug and kiss.

"Well, it's good to see you too, Finn!" she said, giggling at his enthusiasm. "Are you here looking for Gabe?"

"No, I've come looking for you to take you fishing. Gabe tells me you are quite the angler, and I want to see so for myself," he said as he chuckled." Now go get yourself a hat, and let's get going!" She looked at Gabe, who smiled and shrugged his shoulders.

"Um, I-I don't know, do you mean now, right now?" she asked.

"Yes, of course, right now!" he said. "I thought you big city girls were supposed to be spontaneous and all that. Besides, why would you want to hang around here with him while he does all this?" he said as he waved his hat around." Looks pretty boring to me."

Gabe chuckled and shook his head. With that, Kennedy giggled and set off to the bedroom to change.

Finn and Kennedy sat in the shade of the overhang of trees along the riverbank, quietly casting toward a big hole where Finn told her the catfish hung out. She'd already caught two fish to his one, and she'd laughed at how excited he got each time she'd gotten one on the line. The day was hot and still, and the cicadas were making their steady drone. Aside from the occasional kerplunk of a cast, it was otherwise quiet.

"So," Finn said, "you and Gabe figuring it out?"

"What?" she said as she baited her empty hook. "Figuring what out?"

"You know," Finn said as he made another cast to the other side of the hole.

"No, I don't know. What are you talking about?"

"Don't play dumb with me, Kenny; you know what I'm talking about." She knew, but she didn't want to talk about it. She made another cast and let out a heavy sigh.

"There doesn't seem to be anything to figure out," she said, finally. "I don't think he's interested in being more than just friends."

Finn let out a laugh and shook his head. "That, my dear girl, is where I am sure you are wrong."

"Why do you say that?" she asked." I've put myself out there a couple of times with him." She felt the hurt and humiliation welling back up inside her.

"Listen," Finn said, "the old boy's got some hang-ups; I'll give you that. But he's red-blooded if you know what I mean. Just in case you might be worried about that."

It was Kennedy's turn to laugh. "No," she said with a chuckle, "I wasn't worried about that."

"Well, you know, when you're 38 and still single, people tend to talk and all that…" he said as he chuckled.

They were quiet for a while as they both concentrated on their fishing and thought about things.

"I've known him since he was a little boy," he began." He's a grown man now, but I still feel a little protective of him. I promised his daddy before he died that I'd always look after him. He went off to war as a young buck, strong and ready to take on the world. He came back home more than a little broken. Saw things over there no man should ever have to see. They gave him the Medal of Honor as if that could heal him." Finn paused, looked down, and shook his head. "He's got nobody, you know. He lost his mama and daddy both in a short time, not long after he got back. He's got a sister somewhere, but she hasn't been in touch with him in years." Finn paused for a minute and took a deep breath." He's a good man, Kenny; he's just been closed off for so long he doesn't know how to turn the spigot back on. I may be an old fool, but I think I know a good match when I see one. I suspect you've got some demons of your own, but I've seen how he looks at you and how you look at him. Don't give up on him, Kenny, and don't give up on yourself either."

Kennedy felt like her heart would wrench right out of her chest. She'd heard a little of what Finn had told her before, but the detail was excruciating for her. Finn, being the gentleman he was, pretended not to notice as she wiped away the tears for a while. And, as strange as it was, it was comforting to be with him as she grieved for Gabe's past. She felt selfish. Yes, she had been through a horrible tragedy but so had he, and she had focused on herself. After a little while, Finn packed up the fishing gear and got the boat ready for their ride home. Finally, he turned to her and said, in a tender voice," Come on, darlin', let's get you home now."

When Finn got Kennedy back to the house, Gabe's truck was gone. *Probably for the better*, he thought. She still seemed somewhat emotional on the way home, and Gabe would not be happy with him if he knew he'd upset her.

It was difficult for him to sit by and watch her cry, but the talk was necessary both for him and her. He knew they were a perfect match, and he would have never forgiven himself if he hadn't at least tried to bring the two together. She needed to hear and understand more about Gabe and his fears and doubts about himself. He had confided in Finn the evening he'd declined her invitation when he stopped in for a whisky. This girl had gotten a hold of Gabe's heart; he just didn't know how to release it to her.

Finn was not one to meddle, he had always believed it was better to live and let be, and he'd thought long and hard before talking to Kennedy about any of it. But he had seen the longing and frustration in Gabe's eyes and her haunting sadness. He felt God had put them together here at the Oasis for a reason.

If he were honest with himself, his reasons were not unselfish. Gabe was like a son to him, and Kennedy conjured up images of what his daughter might look like even though they would not be the same age. And sometimes, he could imagine it was her, falling back into his life by pure happenstance.

He had met Margaret soon after he turned 21 in the summer after he graduated from college in Atlanta. Introduced by a mutual friend, they fell quickly and madly in love. It was a fiery and intense relationship; they were married only a few months after meeting. Margaret had wanted nothing more than a home to keep and a child to raise, but Finn had a thirst for adventure he could not deny. His life had been colorful, having backpacked all over the world on school breaks and during summers. At fourteen, he got his private pilot's license and flew endless hours by himself in his dad's Piper Cub. As a champion amateur boxer, he had gone to Mexico City in 1968 to compete in the Summer Olympic Games, barely missing a medal by a point. And by growing up in rural North Florida, he had become an expert with a rifle, a bow, and a Bowie knife by the time he was a young teenager. Settling down in the suburbs of Atlanta held no appeal for him, but Margaret, now pregnant, wanted to stay in her hometown and near her family.

With his knowledge of aviation and his aeronautical engineering degree, Finn landed a job with an aerospace company in the Atlanta area. While the job was lucrative, it was a desk job and stifling for Finn, who longed for adventure and the outdoors.

When Finn left his steady paycheck and go into aircraft brokerage, baby Emily was three years old. Margaret was unhappy as the work would involve a lot of traveling for Finn, and the risks of starting a business were frightening to her. By then, she had grown accustomed to a comfortable, suburban lifestyle. The first few months were difficult as Finn struggled to get on his feet, but by the end of the first year, he was doing well. His marriage, however, was not. He found he was happier on the road than at home, though he missed his daughter. Every time he came home, Margaret seemed more unhappy, and he was at a loss as to what to do about it. Finally, Finn moved out of their home in Atlanta and took an apartment nearby. That way, he could still see little Emily when he was in town, which, over the next year, became less and less often. As his business grew and became more lucrative, he thought he could slow down and spend more time with her, but it never seemed to work out that way.

One cold morning, he got a phone call while he was getting ready to leave his hotel room in Chicago. Margaret's mother had found her dead of a stroke on their bedroom floor in their Atlanta home. Luckily, Emily had been at kindergarten and not with her mother in the house when it happened. Finn rushed back to Atlanta to be with his daughter and bury his wife. He moved back into the house, thinking it would be the best thing for Emily, but he struggled with the memories and trying to run the business and care for a six-year-old. It was a dark time for him as he suffered through the guilt and the loss. Though they hadn't lived under the same roof for the last couple of years, he still loved her.

The next few months were tumultuous as Margaret's parents pressured Finn to let little Emily come and live with them. Giving up his daughter was the last thing he wanted but the nature of his business, with the travel, made it difficult, as it seemed they were constantly shuffling Emily back and forth. Finally, Finn agreed to let Emily live with them full-time, and he would visit with her when he was in Atlanta. In his heart of hearts, the arrangement crushed him, but he was also realistic and knew that it was probably the best decision for Emily to have a stable home with her grandparents. She adored them and they, her.

Over the years, he saw her less and less, especially when she left for college in Southern California. For a few years, they would exchange cards and gifts, by mail, on birthdays and holidays, but that went to a trickle and then stopped altogether quite a few years ago. The cards he sent eventually started to be returned to him as "addressee unknown," and he lost track of her after her grandparents passed away. As it stood now, he had not heard from her in a decade.

Finn had bought the cabin in the Oasis many years before as a place to hunt and get away on weekends, but, as time went by, he spent more time there. He had maintained a home in Atlanta for Emily's sake more than anything, but he sold it after she left for college. When he retired and sold his business, he moved down to the cabin full-time.

He'd done well with his business, particularly in the final years, as the sale prices of the airplanes he sold increased and his commission checks had gotten bigger. When he sold the business, he added a sizable amount of money to his nest egg and established a large trust for Emily. As part of his will, he'd allocated money for whatever resources were needed to find her. He'd thought about looking for her many times over the last few years but figured it wasn't right to go looking for someone who, so clearly, didn't want to be found.

Chapter Seven

"Love is patient, love is kind. It does not envy, it does not boast, it is not proud. It does not dishonor others, it is not self-seeking. It is not easily angered, it keeps no record of wrongs. Love does not delight in evil but rejoices with the truth. It always protects, always trusts, always hopes, always perseveres." 1 Corinthians 13:4-7

The next morning Gabe found Kennedy walking along the riverfront with a cup in hand. He waved and when she turned and started up toward the house, he saw a mix of expressions on her face. Most of all, she looked tired. He had suspected she was having trouble sleeping for some time, though she had not confided in him about it. Aside from fatigue, he also saw a new, softer expression but had no idea what it meant. She was a girl of many colors, of that he was sure.

"Coffee is on," she said in a soft, sleepy voice when she reached the porch. He went to the kitchen and poured himself a cup. As he stood there for a moment and looked around the little cabin, he realized how warm and inviting it had become. It was starting to feel like her, and he wanted to spend more time there. The old farmhouse he lived in was too big for one person. It was a house built for a family, and with only him there, it was lonely and echoey.

He stepped out onto the porch and looked out toward the river. It was a bright, clear morning, and the dew glistening on the grass looked like ice. It was early, so the sun had not yet breached the high tops of the cypress trees, so while it was still a comfortable temperature, he suspected the day would be hot.

"Beautiful morning," he said as he sat down in the chair beside her.

"Mmmmm," she said not taking her eyes off the view. "My osprey has come to visit again. See him there in the tree?"

Gabe nodded but then turned to look at her. "You ok?" he said. "You look tired."

"I am," she said. "I didn't sleep well."

He was surprised at the confession. She was usually so guarded with him.

"How was your fishing excursion with Finn?" he said, trying to lighten the mood.

"It was nice," she said, hiding the emotions Finn had stirred up in her. "He took me to a good spot."

"Who caught the most fish?" Gabe asked as he took a sip of his coffee.

"I did." She laughed, and Gabe was relieved to see her mood shift to a happier, lighter one.

"Of course you did," he said, almost muttering it to himself. They sat quietly for a moment listening to the birds and the crickets. "Should have everything finished up early today. Tonight you'll be able to cool the place down with the mini splits. I'll take those old window units out for you this afternoon."

She turned and smiled at him. There was something so comforting about the way he looked after her. Even though she had hired him to do the work, there was a caring that showed in everything he did. She wasn't sure if it was because he had feelings for her, maybe he was this way with all of his clients, but she hoped it was. She'd felt it from the moment she'd met him on the road. She felt protected and safe with him.

She took a minute to admire his profile. Deep in thought, he sat staring out at the river, rubbing his chin. She wondered if he was thinking about her or just what he needed to do for the day.

"Kennedy," he said without taking his eyes off the view, " how would you feel about heading to the coast this afternoon?"

"The coast?" she asked.

"Yeah," he said, "I could use a break, and I should be able to finish up early. We could head over early afternoon; it's not a long drive. Maybe eat a late lunch or an early dinner," he said without looking at her.

"That sounds nice, Gabe. I think I would like that." He turned to her and smiled; she thought he looked genuinely happy. She never knew what he was thinking, but his smile seemed authentic. Maybe they were turning a corner. Perhaps this was the start of something new.

"Well," he said, pulling his large frame out of the chair, "if we are going to get out of town early today, I better get busy."

———————————

Kennedy could smell the sea air as they made their way onto the long causeway over the flats that led to Salt Pine Key. It was a different scenery from the river's cool freshness. The smell of the brackish water on the flats and the sights and the sounds of the approaching little coastal town brought back memories of her childhood and the days spent fishing on her father's boat.

When Gabe asked her to go with him to the coast, she hadn't known what to expect, having never spent time in the Big Bend of Florida. Now the approaching coastline, and the little old town nestled into the marsh, made her feel nostalgic about a time gone by, even though she had never been there before.

When Gabe suggested they make the trip over on his motorcycle, it surprised her and gave her a streak of fear. She had never ridden on a bike before but had trusted Gabe and taken on the adventure. She felt her fear slide away as they wound through the countryside, passing by the beautiful farms and through the oak hammocks. The feel of the wind on her face made her feel free and content and being close to Gabe made her feel safe as she nestled against him and held onto his waist. It was an intimacy that was unexpected.

As they entered the town, Gabe slowed the bike and turned left onto the old main street lined with beautiful, quaint turn-of-the-century buildings. Most had been restored and housed various shops, restaurants, and businesses. As they cruised along, she noticed an old, historic hotel with a restaurant and a bar and made a mental note to learn more about it, intrigued by its old Florida architecture. He found a place to park the bike a block over, and they walked the rest of the way down the main street peeking in the store windows and admiring the beautiful old buildings.

"Are you hungry yet?" he asked. "We could grab a beer and a little something now and have dinner a little later if that suits you."

"That sounds perfect," she said as she smiled at him. She was giving herself over to whatever he had planned for the day. Whatever it was, she was sure he had put some thought into it.

They strolled to the end of the main street and then turned onto the footbridge connected to a small island with several waterfront restaurants and watering holes. They ducked into a little place near the end and found a seat on the deck overlooking the blue water of the Gulf of Mexico.

"What a great little town; thank you for bringing me here," she said, smiling up at him.

"I thought you would like it," he said as he gazed out over the gulf. "This little old town has a lot of history. Been through some big storms, too."

"Really?" she said. "I'm surprised there are so many of the old buildings still standing."

"Yeah, they always seem to make it through," he said as he took a swig of his beer. "A big storm hit here at the turn of the century. It did a lot of damage and took a lot of lives, but the people here rebuilt. The fishing over here is great, so that keeps the economy going along with the tourism. There's also a lot of seafood harvested here. Oysters and clams mostly. Do you like raw oysters?"

"Mmm, yes," she said, her eyes sparkling, "I love them."

Gabe called the waitress over and ordered a couple dozen to share and two more beers. "The local oysters here are small but very tasty," he said, "but I like them that way."

Kennedy smiled and nodded, and they were quiet for a few minutes as they watched a pod of dolphins feed a few hundred feet offshore.

"I forgot to ask you," Gabe said. "what did you find out about the property at the courthouse?"

"Oh nothing, actually, the historical records office is closed until the end of the month. The little lady that runs it is up in Georgia visiting her family," she said with a frown.

"Oh," he said. "Well, I asked Finn what he knew about it, and he did have some info. He said he was sure the Pioneer family built the cabin after they settled here. He guessed around 1900 or so. The family used to own all the land that the Oasis sits on now, but they sold most of it at some point. The family held your property until maybe the early 1990s when old man Willer bought the place."

"Wow, that's interesting. So I'm only the third owner then?" she asked.

"It would seem so," he said as he cleared the table between them to make room for the oysters. "It will be interesting to learn what Miss Olivia knows about it."

"Yes, it will," she said. "I can't wait to meet her. She sounds like such an interesting person."

"I would say that's an understatement, Kennedy," Gabe said with a laugh. She laughed with him, enjoying his good mood.

The oysters were ice-cold and delicious, and while they ate, they watched the water and the fishing boats coming in and out. She thought things seemed to be getting easier between them, and she knew her attraction to him was growing. It thrilled her and scared her to death, especially since she wasn't sure how he felt about her. Though Finn had been encouraging, she was waiting for a definitive sign he was interested in her past friendship and casual lunches. She felt so close to him, especially in moments like this, but there was still a line between them they had yet to cross. She realized at that moment that she'd been staring at the water too long, lost in thought, and maybe he had noticed. She shifted in her seat and tried to change her train of thought.

"Are you getting restless?" he said, looking over at her." You wanna go?"

"Oh no," she said softly." I could sit here all day and look at this view." She had stopped just sort of saying *with you,* but it was what was in her heart. He seemed to sense this, and when he smiled at her as his eyes seemed to say *me too.*

Gabe had been glad when Kennedy wanted to ride over to the coast with him as he hoped it would give them some uninterrupted time together. He so desperately wanted to get closer to her, but he was still struggling with the fear she would see his vulnerabilities once she saw past his tough exterior.

He'd been surprised when she'd willingly and eagerly gotten on the bike, especially when she'd told him she'd never been on one. He'd needed the wind therapy of the ride to blow out the cobwebs that the persistent memories left there. Having her in such proximity to him had been a bonus.

He wondered how long he could keep her at arm's length while he figured out how to let his guard down. He could feel her leaning in emotionally and he had hurt her when he'd declined her invitation for a drink. He just couldn't figure out how to move forward. He wanted to, and he hoped she wouldn't give up before he could give her more of himself.

Once they had gotten to the coast, he had decided on a nice dinner at the historic hotel in town. The food there was as spectacular as the atmosphere, which was magical and romantic. He hoped it would go a long way past the casual lunches to let her know she meant more to him than just a friend.

He was content to sit with her watching the gulls and the dolphins, her profile looking beautiful with the reflection of the water dancing across her perfect features. When she turned and smiled at him, he could feel she was too.

The old hotel, built in the mid-1800s, had a colorful past. From its beginnings as a general store to its stint as a brothel, the old building built from ground oyster shells, limestone, and heart of pine beams had weathered the years and the storms with grace.

100

Kennedy wandered around the small lobby peering up at the old pictures on the walls and marveling at the town's history and the hotel itself. The majestic old Florida gem had stood through the Civil War, the big unnamed hurricane of 1897, the Roaring 20s, Prohibition, and the Great Depression.

Gabe had been talking to the hotel owner while she explored the impressive lobby. In the corner, the owner had fashioned a tiny little boutique that Kennedy found interesting. If she'd had the time, she would have shopped a little longer. The little place had a collection of small art, jewelry, and trinkets from the local artists in the little key

"We've got about a half an hour until they can seat us. Want to have a drink at the bar while we wait?" Gabe said when he found her in the little shop.

"That sounds wonderful," she said, putting back the piece of jewelry she had been admiring.

They found a quiet table in the corner of the bar, where she was mesmerized by the beautiful, old photographs that covered the walls. She guessed they were at least 100 years old by the fading and the yellowing, but they were still interesting and spectacular.

"What would you like to drink?" Gabe asked.

"Surprise me," she said with a twinkle in her eye as the waiter approached them.

"Two Old Fashioned cocktails with a twist," he said as he held up two fingers.

Kennedy could not conceal her surprise or delight, and when Gabe saw her broad smile, he cocked his head.

"How could you have possibly known?" Kennedy asked.

"Known what?" he said, confused.

"Known that that was my favorite drink, right down to the twist," she said, still in disbelief.

"I didn't," he said. "It just seemed to suit the moment." He sat back in his chair, smiling at her. They looked at each other, letting the moment's sweetness settle in. The waiter brought their drinks and they sipped them, enjoying the good mood and atmosphere. "Listen," he said, "when I decided to bring the bike over, I hadn't planned to stay this late or to do much of this," he said, pointing to his drink. "So, I got us a couple of rooms here at the hotel. It's not safe for us to ride back tonight. I hope that's ok and I haven't overstepped my bounds," he said as he slid a room key across the table toward her. She picked up the key and turned it over in her hands, the emotion of the confession hanging in the air.

"No, of course not," she said. "I appreciate that you are looking out for me and uh…us. It's fine, great, actually. I read a little about the hotel in the lobby. It's haunted, you know," she said, teasing him.

"Oh, well, it's going to take a pretty strong spirit to keep up with that," he said, laughing and pointing to his Old Fashioned. "At least we can relax and maybe have some wine with dinner. The food here is really good."

The dining room of the old hotel was like a throwback in time. The colors were soft and tropical, with a mix of greens and creams complemented by the candlelight and the white linen tablecloths. Tall eureka palms graced the corners, and the old, dark, reddish pine on the floors made for a warm and rich atmosphere. The service was in old Southern style, attentive but not intrusive, impeccable and crisp but almost unnoticed. And the food was delectable in every way.

Gabe and Kennedy exchanged stories and laughs, the wine loosening things up and making the conversation flow easier and less inhibited. She hadn't realized how much of herself she had been holding back, but Gabe seemed to enjoy seeing more of her, and she was excited to see him laugh more and relax with her. She was melancholy when the evening was winding down. This trip was the closest they had ever gotten to taking their relationship to the next level, and she didn't want it to end.

They climbed the stairs from the lobby to find their rooms and were surprised to find a central sitting room upstairs with more old photographs. They quietly, so as not to disturb the other guests, walked around the common area studying the photos that depicted a time gone by on the little key. Fishing scenes and little homesteads reminiscent of the town's beginnings were the subjects, and the details were quite interesting. They were both reluctant to end the night, but when Kennedy found herself near the door to her room, she turned to Gabe to say goodnight. He hung back a little, then walked to her and put his arms around her. She involuntarily tensed and hoped he didn't notice; she wasn't sure what was about to happen.

"This has been the best day," he whispered." It was the best day for me in a while. Thank you for coming over here with me."

"Thank you for bringing me with you. It was a good day for me too," she whispered back as the tears welled up in her eyes.

They hung on to each other for a brief minute; then, he pulled away. When he saw the tears in her eyes, his heart wrenched, and he had to look away.

"Well," he said. "Sleep well. I'll come to get you for breakfast around nine?"

"Yes, perfect," she said as he walked away." Sleep well, too."

When she heard his door softly close, she wanted nothing more than to run to him and take away the pain and longing in his eyes, but while she knew this day had been a beginning, she also knew they had a long way to go.

Gabe laid awake in the old antique bed, resisting the wine's pull toward sleep. Knowing she was only a room away was bittersweet. It felt good to have her close where he could protect her, but knowing she was out of his reach was difficult. He hadn't expected the emotions he felt as he left her at her door, and the tears he had seen in her eyes had reflected his own raw feelings. As broken as they both were, they seemed to understand each other.

In the old days, it would have been easy for him to seduce her. With her vulnerability and her obvious attraction to him, he could have, with little effort, charmed his way into bed with her. And, if he were honest with himself, his inherent male need for a woman, especially this woman, was pulling at him. But she was too good for that. And that she was broken somehow made the thought of taking advantage of her repulsive. She was worth waiting for; they were worth waiting for.

He worried that she would grow weary of his hesitation, as noble as it was, and mistake it for indifference. Walking the thin line between was excruciating for him. He wanted nothing more than to dive headlong into a relationship with her but knew that doing so before they both were ready would be certain doom. No, it was better to wait.

He'd been hoping for a moment where he could be honest with her about his feelings and ask her for her patience, but it hadn't come. Tonight they had come close, yet he had stopped short; the restaurant was too public, and the moment at the door was too overwhelming. And while his heart was aching for this woman, his mind challenged him with doubts. Could he ever be whole enough to give himself over to her? Would he ever be enough of a man to fulfill all that she needed? He was smart enough to know that a woman needed more than just physical protection. She would need the intimacy of his heart, the wholeness of his being, and the trust he could stand strong for her. He wasn't sure he could give all those things, at least not yet.

As sleep closed in around him, he could hear the distant barking of the wolves. But instead of the dread he usually felt, he was filled with a new resolve. The day had been too good, and the memory of her smile was too sweet. In his mind, he stood strong, swords crossed, ready to defend against the onslaught. He would not let them in tonight.

When Gabe dropped her off at the cabin, she had felt a little sad but also a little excited at what might lie ahead for them. He had tried to show her that he did have feelings for her, and, though it was a baby step, she realized that she was grateful for the slow pace of their relationship. She wasn't ready, and clearly, he wasn't either. What they had was probably the best they could hope for right now.

When she'd opened her door that morning at the hotel, a small gift bag was hanging on the doorknob. Inside was a piece of jewelry she had admired in the boutique the evening before. It was a sterling silver charm bracelet with a heart, a cross, and an anchor, each with a tiny precious stone. In the bag, the note read: *Something to remind you of our day at the coast together - Gabe*

The gift meant the world to her. She realized this man was struggling and fighting his demons to see his way clear to having a relationship with her. Even with her own demons to conquer, she was determined to give him the chance.

The cabin was cool and dry thanks to the new air conditioning, and she already felt a new freshness there that she hadn't felt before. The humidity of North Florida had made the cabin smell musty with a touch of mildew, and she was happy that it was already diminishing. She was looking forward to the possibility of a better night's sleep with the cooler temperatures. Sleeping through the night had been an issue for her lately.

She was working in the kitchen, moving things out of the way for Gabe to start the work there, when she heard the rumble of a truck pull up in her driveway. Peeking out the window, she saw Finn get out of his truck and head toward her door.

"Well, hello there, Kennedy!" he said as she swung the door open.

"Hey, Finn," she said with a smile. " How are you today?"

"I'm mighty fine, Kenny, mighty fine. I've come to ask you to join me for dinner this evening at Miller's for their Friday night fish fry. Afterward, I'm hoping to talk you into some drinks and dancing. What do ya 'say?" he asked as he held his feathered fedora over his heart.

"Well, that sounds lovely, Finn; I'd love to," she said with a big smile.

"Wonderful!" he said as he turned to go. "Oh, I also spoke with Gabe about it, and he's finishing up a big order for the sawmill this afternoon. He might not make it for dinner, but he said he will try to get on up there a little later."

"Ok," she said. "Sounds like a plan."

Finn waved his hat and called over his shoulder as he pulled the old Ford around in the driveway. "I'll pick you up, Kenny! Six sharp!" And in a cloud of dust, he was gone.

———————

Kennedy could barely believe her eyes when Finn pulled his truck into the parking lot at Miller's. Cars packed the lot of the little fish camp and its front deck was nearly spilling over with people. The music was so loud she could hear it before she even got the car door open.

They parked the truck near the back and walked through the lime rock parking lot to the side door, where Finn held it open for her. They found a place to sit near the end of the bar, and as Finn ordered a whiskey for himself and a beer for her, she noticed how he seemed to know everyone in the place by name. She also noticed the eyes upon her and the wondering glances as to who she might be. Unlike the restaurant, though, she didn't feel uncomfortable with it. It seemed like normal curiosity from people who weren't used to seeing new faces in their regular haunts.

She was excited to be out somewhere on a Friday night. It was a humble place, but Miller's seemed to have a charm that appealed to her. She could see why it was so popular with the locals though she was sure the place had seen its fair share of melodramas. Every local hangout had its own distinct little culture, and she suspected Miller's was no different.

The catfish dinner was as delicious as she remembered it when Gabe brought her there for lunch, and she and Finn had a lively conversation while they ate. She told him about her trip to the coast with Gabe, and he seemed happy at the news they had spent some alone time together, especially the intimate dinner they had shared at the old hotel.

Soon, the music got louder as the place transitioned from the dinner hour to the social scene. The activity on the pool tables and the dart boards picked up, and a few couples were out on the dance floor. Finn danced with her for a couple of songs, and she was impressed with his moves though none were as elegant as the smooth waltz he guided her through to a slow Sinatra song. She could follow him easily, having attended many cotillions in her day, but as a lead, he was pure perfection.

The bar was now three deep and getting louder with conversation and music. The day had turned to night, and she noticed the beer signs and cafe lights gave the porch a soft glow. It was then that she saw Gabe standing near the end, talking to a young woman. She was talking to him intently, and he was leaning in so he could hear her better, but it was the look on his face that struck her. It was a look of suppressed pain yet with a caring she could tell was deep and genuine. As she watched them, she saw Gabe put his hand on her shoulder and draw her to him, his other hand cradling her head to his chest. He closed his eyes for a minute, then bent to kiss the top of her head, and she watched him hold her until she couldn't bear it another second. She turned to Finn, who was in a lively conversation with a friend, and put a hand on his arm when there was a lull.

"I was wondering if you could take me home now," she said with as much composure as she could.

"Sure, darlin' is there anything wrong?" he asked as the concern clouded over his expression.

"Oh, nothing's wrong, I'm a little tired and need to get up early tomorrow morning. I have an appointment in town," she lied.

"Ok, give me a minute and we'll go," he said as he waved down the bartender. As Finn paid the bill, she glanced back at the corner of the porch, but Gabe and the woman were gone. She glanced around the bar, but she didn't see them anywhere. It was almost more painful to wonder where they had gone than it had been to see them standing there together.

"Ready?" Finn said as he held out his hand to help her off the barstool. "You sure there's nothing wrong, Kenny?" he asked as he tilted his head and looked straight into her eyes.

"I'm sure," she said as she shoved her hands into her pockets. "Just tired, that's all."

Back at the cabin, she was consumed in emotion, hurt being the primary one. She just didn't understand. She felt like such a fool. Here she was, falling head over heels in love with this man who was clearly already in love with someone else. She was sure, now, that was why he was so reluctant to move forward with anything between them. What she had seen and the emotions that passed between Gabe and this woman were undeniable. He should have told her even if he were parting ways with this woman. Letting her think he was unentangled and available was wrong and cruel. She was more than just hurt; she was angry.

She stormed to the kitchen and yanked open the refrigerator door. As she pulled out a bottle of wine, she thought better of it, put it back, and went to the cabinet in the living room where she had set up a little bar. Flipping over a crystal tumbler, she angrily filled it halfway with bourbon, looked at it to build her courage, then took a big swig. She coughed, wiped her mouth, and headed to the kitchen for some ice. Even in her unhinged state, she realized drinking bourbon, neat, alone, over a man, was a bridge too far.

She wandered around the cabin, trying to pace off the emotional energy of the situation. Hard as she tried, she could not get the scene out of her mind. The sight of Gabe holding the young woman tore at her insides, and it would be a long time before she could think of it without the stabbing pain she felt now. It was then and there that she realized that no matter how hard her heart had tried not to let it happen, she had fallen in love with him, and now, it seemed, she was going to lose him too.

Chapter Eight

"You have been a refuge for the poor, a refuge for the needy in their distress, a shelter from the storm and a shade from the heat. For the breath of the ruthless is like a storm driving against a wall." Isaiah 25:4

Gabe was surprised when he got to the cabin the next morning to start work and Kennedy was nowhere in sight. Her Jeep was behind the house, so he assumed she was home, but he didn't find her on the front porch as usual, and there was no familiar smell of brewed coffee in the air. Alarmed, he tapped softly on the door and tried the handle on the back door. It was unlocked, and he cracked it slightly and called her name.

"Come in," she answered.

Confused, he tentatively walked into the cabin and found her sitting at the desk in her room, her back to him. "Good morning," he said. "Is everything ok?"

"Yes, fine," she said, not turning toward him. "I got everything out of your way in the kitchen. So you should be able to get started in there. I'm working on some things in here today, just paperwork and stuff, so if you wouldn't mind, will you shut my door, please?"

"Sure, ok," he said. "You're sure everything's…"

"I'm fine, Gabe. I just have some things I need to get done," she said, cutting him off. She finally turned to look at him, and he could see a range of emotions there, but what bothered him the most was the detachment he saw in her eyes. He held up his hand as if to say *ok, I got it*. Something had happened since the last time he saw her, but he could not imagine what it was. He decided not to press and quietly closed her door.

The next hour was spent in misery as he worked, hearing nothing from her from behind the closed door. He made an excuse to coax her out of the bedroom to get to the bottom of what was going on.

He tapped lightly on her door. "Kennedy, sorry to disturb you, but I have questions about a few things in the kitchen. Could you come out for a few minutes so we can talk?" At first, there was no response, then the door opened slowly, and she walked past him into the kitchen and got a pitcher of tea out of the refrigerator.

"Do you want some tea?" she asked in a calm, flat voice.

"Sure," he said, not wanting to be controversial. "Hey, I went to Miller's last night but didn't see you guys. Did y'all end up not going?" he asked, trying to normalize things between them.

"No, we went. We just left early," she said, still not looking him in the eye. "Did you stay long?" she asked, an apparent edge in her voice.

"Not long," he said. "Wasn't very fun or interesting when I realized you guys weren't there," he said with a smile, hoping to soften her up. She looked at him for a long moment, analyzing his response.

"Really?" she said, the sarcasm dripping off her words. "It looked to me like you found at least *something* you thought was interesting." She breezed past him with her tea, went out to the rockers on the porch, and sat down hard, clearly angry and upset.

Gabe was confused about what was happening, and his patience was wearing thin. If she had something to say to him, he wished she would come out with it. It had been a long time since he'd had a situation like this with a woman, and he had forgotten how exasperating women could be when they were angry. He walked out onto the porch and took a deep breath.

"Look, Kennedy," he said, his voice measured and calm. "I don't know what's happening here, but if you are upset with me, I'd like to know why."

She was silent for a moment, then turned to look at him. "It would just have been a lot easier if you'd been honest with me," she said, her eyes full of hurt and betrayal," just a lot easier."

Suddenly, it hit him, and he knew what she was talking about. When she saw the light dawn in his eyes, she got up from her chair, knowing the truth was coming but not ready to hear it.

"Wait a minute, Kennedy, wait just a damn minute. I can explain," he said, catching her by the arm before she could get too far from him.

"You don't have to explain anything to me, Gabe. You have no obligation to me. You are free to do what you want and see who you want. As it stands right now, we are just friends, and you are the guy who works on my house, nothing more," she said as the tears welled up in her eyes. "I was foolish to think it might someday be more than that, but I guess not." She tried to withdraw from him, but he pulled her to him and grabbed her by the shoulders, looking her directly in the eyes.

"Are you going to let me explain?" he said, trying to keep his anger in check.

"You don't have to!" she said, her voice just below a shout.

"I want to, and I think I deserve to. I have never been anything but honest with you, Kennedy. As God as my witness, I have never tried to deceive you."

They were quiet for a minute, breathing hard and trying to get a hold of their emotions.

"I'm a Veteran, Kennedy; I think you know that," he began. "I belong to a group of Vets that get together to talk and help each other cope. It's hard, Kennedy, we struggle every day but talking helps, so we meet to do that and try to help each other. The girl you saw me with is Miller's granddaughter. She was only 12 when she found her daddy, who'd put a gun to his head and taken his life because he couldn't cope anymore. A few of the guys and I sort of took her and her mama under our wing, and a couple of years ago, she started coming to our group. Yesterday was a tough day for her. She'd found some letters he'd written home, and they were about her and all his hopes and dreams for her. It put her in a tailspin. She's only 18 years old, Kennedy; she could be my daughter." He released her as he finished, put his head down, and walked away from her.

"Gabe, I - I'm…" she stuttered but stopped talking when he put his hand up to silence her.

He stood for a minute with his back to her, composing himself and his thoughts. Finally, he turned and looked at her for a long moment.

"I'm not good at this, Kennedy, I'll admit that. It's been a long time since I've had a relationship with a woman and opening myself up to you is hard. To be honest, I'm afraid. I'm afraid you'll see too much and won't like what you see. I'm willing to try, though. For the first time in a long time, I'm willing to try." He stopped for a moment and felt his heart nearly implode when he saw the sadness and regret written on her face. "I will never hurt you, and I'll give you whatever I can. I just don't know how much that is right now. I know you struggle, too; I've seen the pain in your eyes. I don't know why but don't think I don't see it. I just want…I just think we need to take things slow and see how things go. If that isn't enough for you, I completely understand. I won't like it, but I'll understand."

Kennedy stepped toward him and stopped, unsure what to say or do. Gabe reached out a hand and pulled her to him, slowly wrapping his arms around her and holding her tight against his chest. The tenderness of the moment and the raw emotions she saw in Gabe were too much for her, and she couldn't hold back her tears any longer. They stood there for a long time as Gabe held her while she cried. It was excruciating for him to listen to her soft sobs but as sad as it was, it was the most connected he'd felt to another human being in a long time.

Kennedy sat in the rocker on her porch, watching the two artists down by the river work on their pieces. The osprey had come back and circled above, seemingly curious about the two people and their easels at the water's edge. She'd gotten a phone call from Cadence, the art gallery owner, asking if she would allow them to come to her property and paint her view. Adsila had mentioned it was unique and beautiful. She had readily agreed and hoped the plein air artists would capture it as she saw it in the mornings and evenings from her porch. She hoped to, perhaps, buy one of the art pieces if they were successful in doing so.

She could hear Gabe banging away in the kitchen, working on her little renovation there. He'd been at it for several days, and she was thrilled with how it was turning out. It looked fresh and crisp but still held the old charm she loved about the cabin.

Things had been a little different since she'd mistakenly confronted him about the girl. To say she felt foolish and terrible about it was an understatement, but at least it had put all the cards on the table. Now without the doubt and insecurities between them, they seemed able to take a small step forward in their relationship, each more content to let it unfold slowly. There were

114

still mountains of mysteries between them and things they could not talk about yet, but at least they knew where they stood.

The sun was getting low in the sky, and the light the painters depended on was fading. Kennedy watched as they slowly packed their things up for the day and headed toward the house.

"I'm not sure when we will be back to paint again," one of the artists said to Kennedy as she stepped onto the porch. "With the storm possibly heading this way, we may get some rain over the next few days."

"Storm?" Kennedy asked.

"Yes," she said, "there's a storm brewing in the Gulf. Right now, it's just a tropical storm, but they expect it to be a hurricane by tonight."

"Oh," Kennedy said. "I hadn't heard. Seems a bit early in the season for a storm; it's barely June."

"Sure is. Right now, they are predicting it will move up this way in the next few days, but you know how these things go," she said.

Kennedy smiled and nodded. Growing up in Florida, the threat of storms wasn't new to her, nor was their unpredictable nature. There was no sense in getting worried about something that, most likely, would change course.

She said goodbye to the artists and checked on Gabe's progress in the kitchen. She found him with his legs sprawled out across the kitchen floor and the rest of him crammed underneath a cabinet installing her new sink. When she heard the clanging of tools and the mutterings under his breath, she decided it was probably not the best time to bother him. Instead, she decided to find out what the authorities were saying about the storm.

She had decided against putting a television in the cabin. It didn't make sense to her to get away from the city only to bring it back into her living room via a TV. She did, though, have internet installed and a phone line for safety's sake. The internet signal was the only way she could utilize Wi-Fi calling on her cell phone and use her laptop. She thought the landline was a good idea if the power went out.

When she pulled up the National Hurricane Center website and looked at the storm track, it showed the predicted path passing right over the Oasis. She also saw this one was, what Floridians call, a "homegrown" storm, meaning it had not formed out of a tropical wave coming off the African coast but rather right in their own backyard in the Gulf of Mexico. Hurricane Michael, one of only a handful of storms making landfall in Florida as a Category 5, had been such a storm. Michael had grown from a mere tropical depression just south of Florida into a devastating storm that slammed into the Panhandle of Florida just three days later, leaving little to no time for preparation. She knew this was a storm to watch.

"Any news on the storm?" Gabe asked, standing behind her, wiping his hands with a rag.

"Yes," she said as she turned her laptop toward him, "they think it could come right over us. It's just a tropical storm now, but they are predicting it to be a category 2 or 3 when it makes landfall."

"Well," he said." We don't worry too much about winds being this far inland. The biggest threat to us is the rain. Too much, and we could be looking at a flood."

"A flood? Really?" she asked. This had never occurred to her.

"Yeah," he said, "we've had a few throughout the years. You are on pretty high ground here, and you are up on a pier foundation of a few feet, so it's unlikely you will ever get water in the house, but water could certainly surround the house or cut off access to it. That's what happens here in the Oasis, mostly."

"Oh," she said." Is there anything I need to be doing?"

"No, not yet," he said. "Let's just watch it and see. If it looks like we need to start moving things out of the way, don't worry, you'll have lots of help."

Things were not looking good at the ten o'clock advisory from the Hurricane Center. Now a named storm, Hurricane Alene had picked up speed and was heading northeast as a category 2 storm with further development expected. If it stayed on its predicted path, it would come in right at Salt Pine Key and pass just to the west of the Oasis as it made its way toward Georgia. With little to alter its course and current speed, it would now be mere hours before it made landfall.

Almost as soon as she finished reading the advisory, there was a knock at her door, and when she peeked out the window, she saw Gabe's truck in her driveway. She opened the door, and he walked in without hesitation.

"Have you seen the latest advisory?" he asked.

"Yes," she said. "I was just looking at it. It doesn't look good."

"No, it doesn't," he said. "Listen, I can't stay long. Finn and I are going door to door, letting everyone know to meet at the Pavilion in an hour so we can plan. If we wait, this thing will be on us before we know it. We have some older folks out here that will need looking after. I gotta go but come on up there around eleven o'clock."

"No," she said. "I'm coming with you now."

———————

When they arrived at the Pavilion, she was happy to see many cars there. Sometimes it was hard to get people to take these storms seriously, but that did not appear to be the case with this one. The lights were already blazing, and when they came through the open doors, she saw Adsila setting up chairs and went to help her.

When it seemed everyone was there, Gabe got behind the podium to address the crowd:

"Listen up, folks; this storm is shaping up to be a bad one. The National Hurricane Center says they expect it to come on shore as at least a 3, maybe a 4. We are a bit inland, but, as the crow flies, we are less than 60 miles from the coast, so if it's a strong one when it lands, it could still be pretty powerful when it gets here. But, all of us know that flooding is a real concern also, so we need to prepare for both," he said as he addressed the crowd. "I'm going to offer up my barns to park vehicles in and my house for people to use as a storm shelter. The farm is on high ground, and the farmhouse is big and sturdy. I've got generators and a rainwater catchment system I use for the farm. We can take care of a lot of folks up there for a few days if necessary. I don't think we will keep power, and we are all on wells out here, so there could be no water at your homes for a while. I've got plenty of food but feel free to bring some with you if you want to. Bring whatever you need to be comfortable, and please don't forget any medications you may need. If you need help getting yourself there, call one of us, and we will have someone come get you. Don't delay. We've only got about 20 hours until it comes on shore. Let's adjourn now so we can all get busy securing our homes and making plans. Any questions?"

Several minutes later, when everyone was leaving, Gabe found Kennedy outside waiting for him. They got in his truck and started back to her cabin.

"I've been through some hurricanes, so I know what to do at the cabin. Is there anything else I need to do for the flooding?" she asked.

"No," he said," I've got a lot to do tonight to secure the farm and the animals, but I'll be back in the morning to take care of a few things for you and bring you up to the farm."

"Bring me up to the farm?" she asked. "No, I think I'll stay at the cabin. It's old, but it's sturdy, and you said the water would take a couple of days, at least, to rise. I think I would just be in the way at the farm, Gabe. You'll have enough to deal with there as it is."

"Kennedy, I don't want to argue about this right now. I've got a lot to do, and I don't have the energy for it. But, I'll tell you right now that I'm not comfortable with you staying at the cabin by yourself. I'll be down here early in the morning, and we will talk about it then," he said as he pulled up to her back porch.

"Ok," she said as she opened the car door, "good night, then."

He waited till she got the door open, then waved and backed out. She slipped inside and shut the door. She felt terrible for irritating him. He had taken on the responsibility for the community's safety and had a lot on his shoulders. The last thing he needed was any grief from her.

———————

The following day, at the break of dawn, Kennedy stepped out on her porch to a gloomy morning. The low clouds were moving fast as a steady wind was blowing. The air had a" tropical" feel anyone who's been through a hurricane would instantly recognize. She took in the hummingbird feeders and wind-chimes and anything else that was not battened down on the porches. She dragged the rockers into the spare bedroom along with the small tables and potted plants. Within the hour, the porches were bare.

119

She was glad to see that the old shutters were functional, and she closed up the house one by one. She left two open on the front porch so she could see what was happening outside. She saw the old canoe Gabe had retrieved for her by the edge of the water and pulled it farther up into the yard. When she moved it forward, a large water snake slithered up the bank and into the high grass. *Everything is headed for high ground,* she thought. By the time Gabe was expected, the house outside was battened down tight, so she set to work getting organized inside.

She heard his footsteps on the back porch, and when he cracked the door and called her name, she called back to him.

"In here!"

He found her in the bathroom scrubbing out the old clawfoot tub with bleach and detergent and saw she had a caulk gun on the floor next to her cleaning supplies.

"Looks like you know what you are doing," he said with a smile.

"Almost done," she said." There's coffee on in the kitchen."

When she was finished cleaning the tub and had caulked the drain, she found him at the window, looking out over the yard and the river.

"Anything in that shed I need to move?" he asked as he sipped his coffee.

"Not really," she said. "There's an old anchor and some folding chairs. Nothing I'm worried about, though. I did pull the canoe up a bit. Do you think it's up far enough?"

"For now, yes," he said. He looked around and noticed all her preparations. She had a lot of candles set about, the bathtub was ready to be filled with fresh water, and he saw she had a stocked pantry when he'd worked on her kitchen. "Looks like you've made up your mind to stay here, then?" he said as he turned to look at her.

"I'd like to," she said. "I feel safe here."

"I don't like it, Kennedy. If you are here, by yourself, I can't protect you. The thought of that scares me. But you are a grown woman and can make your own decisions. I'm going to ask one more time, though, for you to let me take you up to the farm." He stopped and waited, and when she said nothing, he held up both hands. "Ok then, I don't have time to argue. I've got some older folks I need to get up there. I'll be around to check on you here and there for as long as I can. If you change your mind, please do it soon." He turned to go, then turned back to her and looked her in the eyes for a minute. "Please be careful here, Kennedy. Promise you'll call me if you need me."

She smiled at him. "I will, I promise."

After Gabe left, she busied herself with finishing her preparations. She filled the old claw foot tub, put oil in the lanterns, and double-checked the shutters. Satisfied that she had done all she could, she sat down to check the update on the storm. The latest update was out, and the predicted path of Hurricane Alene had changed little. As it stood now, when she came over the Oasis, the area of heaviest rain, the northeast quadrant, would pass directly over them. They could not have gotten worse news. Rain predictions were a staggering 18"-24" in a mere 24 hours. There would be no escaping a flood now.

To make matters worse, Alene had strengthened to a solid category 4. There was a chance she would slow down and weaken as she approached the coast, but that would only dump more rain. There was no good scenario. The only good news was that Alene was expected to hit at low tide, which would be a blessing to the folks on the coast. They had updated landfall predictions to approximately 8 pm, right at dark. *The bad ones always come at night,* she thought.

As the next few hours passed, the winds steadily picked up, and by 6 pm, they were blowing in earnest. Every so often, the lights would flicker, and she would hold her breath, but they had stayed on so far. She closed the last of the shutters as the chance of something flying through an unprotected window was an increasing threat. As promised, she was being careful.

At 7 pm, she checked the storm path. The Hurricane Center showed Alene close to the coast, just off Salt Pine Key. She knew when the eye-wall came on shore that would be the worst of it. She said a silent prayer for the people there and hoped, somehow, the storm would spare them the devastation predicted. A short time later, the lights flickered and went out, and she reached over, a little panicked, and clicked on the emergency light Gabe had brought her that afternoon. Once she had lit the candles and had the lanterns going, she felt calm again and switched off the emergency light. It was important to save resources now.

She felt that edginess in her joints that some people talk about who have been through hurricanes. Having something to do with the drop in the barometric pressure, it was a known phenomenon. With each passing minute, the winds and the rain seemed to become more intense as the storm advanced toward them. The pelting rain on the tin roof became almost deafening, and the realization that the worst part of the storm was not yet upon them made her doubt the wisdom of her choice to stay at the cabin alone. She thought of Gabe and his insistence she come to the farm and how warm and protected she would feel now if she was there with him. Staying at the cabin had been a stupid decision.

The wind was howling now, whistling through the towering cypress, through the old live oaks, and around the corners and eves of the old cabin. The creaking and the moaning sounds she heard were ominous and frightening to listen to, and now and then, she felt a gust so powerful that she could swear the whole structure moved.

As Alene's eyewall moved on shore, her forward winds raged over the Oasis. Kennedy could hear the snapping of limbs and thunderous rain beating on the roof and the windows. Now and then, something big would land on the roof or batter the side of the cabin. There was nothing left to do but curl up on the old couch and pray.

Chapter Nine

"Trust in the LORD with all your heart and lean not on your own understanding; in all your ways, submit to him, and he will make your paths straight." Proverbs 3:5-6

The banging was loud and relentless, and Kennedy thought that maybe a shutter on the back porch had broken loose and was clattering against the house. She got up to investigate even though she didn't want to leave her cocoon on the couch where she had sat wrapped in a blanket for the last few hours. As she approached the door, she thought she heard her name, and when she got right up against it, she was sure she did. Knowing the wind would blow the door open if she tried to open it, she braced herself against it and slowly turned the knob. As the door cracked open, she saw a hand reach inside and grab the door, holding it fast and allowing it to open just enough so the jacket-clad figure could slip inside.

Gabe was drenched to the core; the rain shedding off his hooded rain jacket made an instant puddle on the floor. His face was red from being beaten by the rain, and his jeans and boots were soaked.

"My God, Gabe, what are you doing?" she said, genuinely alarmed.

"I couldn't stand being up there knowing you were down here by yourself. How are things? Does the cabin seem to be holding up ok?" he asked as he pulled off his jacket.

"I think so. I've heard some pretty strange things over the last couple of hours, but there is no water coming in that I can tell. I'm afraid the little place is taking a beating, though," she said as her face clouded over with sadness. "Anyway, I'm really glad you are here."

He smiled and pulled her to him in a bear hug." I'm glad I'm here too. I was worried about you here. It's pretty bad, but I think we are in the worst of it. If we can get through the next couple of hours, I think we will be ok."

"Let me get you a towel and the jeans and the t-shirt you left here last week when you'd been working under the house. I washed them for you."

She went to the armoire, retrieved his dry clothes and a towel, then returned to the couch and wrapped the blanket around her. Gabe dried himself as best he could, removed his soggy boots, and went to change.

"What's it like out there?" she asked as he sat beside her." Did you see a lot of damage on your way here?" A powerful gust hit the cabin just then, and the roof gave out a loud groan. They looked at each other for a tense moment, but as the moment passed, they both breathed a sigh of relief.

"Yeah, It's not good. I had to navigate my way around several downed trees and limbs, and it looked like some houses had roof damage. We won't know the extent of it until daylight when we can get a better look. The rainfall has been huge, so I'm sure there's a flood coming. My rain gauge at the farm already shows at least 12 inches."

"Oh," she said. "This is terrible. I'm really sad for our little community." Kennedy put her face in her hands and let out a little sob, the stress of the last few hours overtaking her. Gabe moved over next to her and put an arm around her.

"These are strong folks here, Kennedy. We always come through. It will be ok. I promise it will be ok," he said as he rubbed her shoulder. "Hey, If you've got any bourbon, I could really use one about now," he said trying to distract her. She smiled and pointed to the antique cabinet behind the couch where she had set up her bar. He got up, poured a little into two tumblers, and then went to the kitchen for ice.

When he sat back down beside her, and they listened to the pounding rain and wind, Gabe pondered how she had never told him how she came to the Oasis. He had casually asked the question once, but her response had been vague, and he sensed something cataclysmic had happened that brought her there. It had been on his mind since that moment, and he knew it was a significant hurdle for them to get over if they were going to move forward and make something of this connection between them. Whatever it was, it was like a giant chasm between them that needed to be closed.

"Kennedy," he said. "I've been meaning to ask you this for a while, and if you aren't ready to tell me, I understand." He paused as he looked down at her hands and took one between his two. "Something brought you here to the Oasis, to me. My heart tells me it was something that hurt you in a big way. I know, believe me, I know that it's hard to talk about things in the past that are painful. But talking helps; it really does."

She turned to look at him, her eyes full of trepidation and fear. He suspected maybe it was a divorce or a bad break-up, but this girl seemed to have given up everything and arrived here with only what would fit in her car. Where had she come from, and what was she running from? He needed to know. Her bottom lip trembled, and she opened her mouth to speak, but nothing came out. Gabe resisted the urge to shut down the moment and tell her it was ok; she didn't have to tell him. He knew, from experience, that talking about a traumatic event for the first time was the hardest. He waited, holding his breath as she spoke, her voice barely above a whisper.

"I lost them, Gabe, I lost them all…"

"Lost who, sweetie? Who did you lose?" he asked with as much tenderness as he could muster.

"My family…I lost my family," she said as the first tear slid down her cheek. He paused for a minute, giving her a chance to breathe.

"How did you lose them, Kennedy? It's ok, you can tell me," he asked, still not comprehending what she was telling him.

"In the fire…I-I lost them in the fire on my dad's boat. I-I was supposed to be there with them. I-I should have been there with them," she whispered as the dam of emotions broke, and she fell against him, sobbing.

Gabe was stunned by the magnitude of what she had told him. In his wildest speculations, he had never imagined this. Now, everything was making sense. The haunting sadness he had seen in her eyes reflected this profound loss. Now he knew this woman wasn't just running from a tragedy; she was trying to start a whole new life in an unkind world, all alone. He didn't press her for details; they would come later. This was enough for now. It was a start, and as painful as it was, he was glad she had trusted him enough to tell him. His heart broke for her in so many ways as he held her. He knew a little about what she was going through, having lost his parents so close together but he had at least had his chance to say goodbye. And although his sister Sara Lee and he were not close, at least he wasn't all alone in the world. He'd also had the little community that had come together to comfort him and look after him and his buddies from the military to lean on. It appeared that she had no one, and he could not imagine the courage it had taken for her to come here by herself. Suddenly, his troubles seemed to lift from him as he put everything in perspective and comprehended the strength of this woman. Through all that she had been through and was still enduring, she still seemed ready, or at least willing, to give herself over to him, to trust him, and, perhaps, even fall in love with him. Even with knowing the risk of loss and the excruciating pain that would go with it. She had immense courage, and he not only admired her for it, but it also inspired him. At that moment, he realized that she was a gift to him; a precious gift from God who had sent to her to rescue his heart and mind from the demons that tormented him, and that he would never, could never, let her go.

When Kennedy opened her eyes, she first noticed the absence of sound. Looking up, she realized she had been asleep for what seemed like hours, with her head in Gabe's lap. His head was lolled back against the sofa, and his eyes were closed. His hand rested on her shoulder, heavy with sleep. She laid quietly for a moment listening for any noise from the storm, realizing there was none. She took the opportunity to study his features in the soft candle light and saw he had a peacefulness in his expression. It wasn't often that his face didn't reflect the burdens he carried. He looked almost childlike in his sleep, an innocence that the waking hours robbed from him.

She had finally told him, and though it had been painful, she felt that her soul had healed some through the confession. As hard as it was, there was relief in the aftermath. He had let her cry for what seemed like forever as he held her, and she was grateful for his bravery and his kindness. She was realizing how blessed she was that he had come into her life.

Gabe stirred a little and took a deep breath. She didn't move, not wanting to disturb him if he was falling back into sleep. But when she saw his eyes flutter open, she realized this man was constantly vigilant, even in sleep. Somehow he had sensed she was awake.

He peered down at her and gave her a slight smile. "You ok?" he asked, as his hand stroked over her hair. She could only nod and give him a weak smile as his tenderness made her feel emotional all over again. "I think the storm is over," he said. "It's pretty quiet out."

"I think you're right," she said as she sat up." I've been listening for a while, but I haven't heard much. What time is it?"

Gabe checked his watch. "It's five o'clock, too early to check on the storm damage, but I'll head out at first light,"

"Do you want some coffee?" she asked." I've got a French press, and I can heat the water on the gas stove to make a pot."

"Yes," he said. "I'd love some. And I'm going to need it. It's going to be a long day."

He checked his cell phone for a signal and was surprised to find he had a slight one. He dialed Finn, who answered immediately. He'd been worried when Gabe set out into the storm to check on Kennedy. She listened to his side of the conversation and tried to follow it.

"Finn, hey, it's Gabe…Yeah, we're ok. How's everything up there at the farm?... Good, and the generators are running ok?... Ok, that's good. Hey, I'm going to head out of here at daybreak and do a little reconnaissance on the neighborhood. See what kind of an assessment I can get…Yeah, ok, I'll see if I can get to you to pick you up. I'll call you when I'm on the way…Yep, ok."

When he hung up, he turned to Kennedy and caught her smiling at him.

"This little community is lucky to have you, Gabe. You're a good man and a good leader," she said as she leaned on the counter, waiting for the coffee to finish brewing.

"These people are my family, Kennedy. Trust me, I leaned hard on them when my parents passed. They were there for me then, and I'm gonna be here for them now or whenever I'm needed. It's the least I can do for all they've done for me. Listen, I'm gonna walk around a bit outside with a flashlight and see what kind of damage you have. Stay here; I won't be long," he said as he put on his jacket and went out the door.

Kennedy paced around the cabin as she waited for Gabe. She felt tired and thought she might lie down after he left at daybreak to get a little more sleep. The night had been a hard one. She felt a little drained between the fear of the storm and her revelations with Gabe. But deep down, her troubles felt a little lighter, having someone else to help shoulder them.

"Well," Gabe said as he came back through the door. "It isn't pretty. Your property is a mess with lots of downed limbs and debris. You've got a pretty big tree down at the back, but I think we can get around it to get out. The cabin looks pretty good, though, from what I could see, just a little tin peeled back on the porch. I'll take a closer look when I have some light. The river is way up, though, not a good sign. I think we are going to have a pretty big flood. Listen, don't go poking around out there while I'm gone. It's still a little gusty, so there are probably some limbs hanging that could still fall, and with the river coming up fast, the snakes are going to be looking for higher ground. Just stay inside until I get back, ok?"

"Ok, I think I might take a nap while you're gone," she said as she yawned and handed him his coffee. "I'm still a little tired."

Gabe nodded and looked at her closely. She looked tired, and her eyes were still swollen from crying, but there was a peace he could detect, a slight difference from before. He knew that feeling. When the ever-present wolves could be tamed, even for a little while, it was a relief to the soul.

When Gabe finally made it up to the farm, Finn was waiting for him at the gate. He climbed into the truck and turned to him.

"Mornin 'Gabe, what's our little Oasis look like this morning?"

"Well, I haven't been through it all, I was trying to get here to pick you up first, but we've got our hands full, that's for sure." Gabe put the truck in gear and started forward. "Let's go up this way and circle back around and see what we find."

As they slowly drove through the narrow lanes of the Oasis, going door to door checking on residents that stayed in their homes, neither man spoke much, but each made mental notes of the work to be done. There were trees and large limbs down everywhere. Gabe spent some time on the phone with the local power co-op giving them locations of downed power lines and hazards. After they looped around, they passed the Pavilion and were relieved to see that the old tobacco barn looked no worse for the wear. Some clean-up around the grounds was all it needed. Finally, Gabe pulled to a stop and put the truck in park so the men could talk.

"Finn, we need to get organized and get this place cleaned up. We can't expect to get power again until the co-op can get trucks in here."

Finn nodded in agreement. "How many tractors do we have out here in the neighborhood, do you reckon?" he asked.

131

"Let me think," Gabe said. "I've got two up on the farm; you've got one. Mr. Smith and Jim Thomas have one each. There are a couple more, I'm sure. I'd say at least six."

"That's what I was thinking. Just about every man out here has a chainsaw. I think if we organize, we can at least get the roads passable in a few days."

"I agree," Gabe said. "Let's get Adsila to head up getting folks fed some hot meals up at the farm. I've got two large freezers full of venison and another full of beef, and my root cellars are full. I think she can handle that, and she'll have lots of help from the other ladies."

"Ok, then, that sounds good," Finn said. "Take me back to the farm so I can get my truck, and we'll start rounding up men and equipment." He glanced at his watch, "What do ya say we have every able-bodied man meet at the Pavilion at 9 am. Then we can divide up the work and get started."

Gabe nodded, turned the truck around, and started back to the farm. When they had picked their way through the debris and the downed trees, he pulled up to the gate. Gabe turned to the older man and stuck out his hand to him, thanking God he could rely on Finn.

"Good plan, Finn, I'll see you at nine."

Not long before the meeting, Gabe swung by Kennedy's cabin and picked her up. He had her pack a bag with enough clothes for a couple of days and took her up to the farm to settle her into the guest house. Staying in the cabin in the heat with no water or electricity would be miserable. At least on the farm, she would be comfortable, and she could help Adsila, and the other ladies feed the community. By mid-morning, the Oasis was alive with the sounds of tractors rumbling, chainsaws buzzing, and the shouts of the men hard at work. It was a race against time as the flood waters were rising and would eventually choke off some access to parts of the community. And, as is typical after hurricanes, and a blessing, the men worked in good weather as the storm took the clouds and the humidity with it when it left.

Kennedy did her best to help the ladies prepare the food. Not being much of a cook, she could only get them things as needed, chop vegetables and help organize. By the afternoon, they had a hot meal line set up and were ready to serve the neighbors and the weary men who straggled in from the roads, dirty and exhausted. She tried not to dwell on the devastation she'd seen on the way to the farm. Instead, the kindness and generosity she saw among the neighbors in the little community inspired her.

A few days later, Kennedy asked Gabe to take her back to the cabin to retrieve a few things. Since restoring power might take a while, she needed more clothes and a few personal items. She also needed to clean out her refrigerator. There wasn't much in there or the freezer, but she didn't want to come home to a refrigerator full of smelly, spoiled food.

When he pulled down her driveway, she was surprised to see the big tree had been cleared, and most of the debris around the property was gone. Gabe told her he'd had a couple of the neighborhood kids pick up the small stuff, and he'd cut up and moved the tree to a pile in the back of the property. They would burn it when things dried out.

What surprised her the most was how high the water was. When she walked out onto the front porch, she saw it was lapping at her front steps, and her entire front yard was submerged. The little lean-to had disappeared under the water nearly black from the flood.

"Oh, Gabe," she said, a little overwhelmed. "Is it going to get any higher?"

"A little but not too much," he said. "And it should start receding in the next few days. The only good thing about these hurricane floods is they don't usually last long. The water comes downstream and gets gone pretty quick."

"It's just surreal to see it this high. I could have never imagined it," she said, staring out over the broad swath of water.

"It's definitely a sight to see," he said. "Your canoe is tied off over there in the side yard. I pulled it up and out of the way a couple of days ago."

"Oh, thank you," she said. "I'd forgotten all about it."

They were quiet for a few minutes as they gazed out over the expanse of water. She noticed the osprey was back at work, circling overhead and making his familiar calls, and was happy to see he had weathered the storm ok. The water was alive with activity, every living thing being displaced and trying to find a new habitat. She watched as a water snake swam from one tree to the next and wondered if it was the same one she had seen a few days ago.

"One thing, Kennedy," Gabe said. "Don't ever wade around in that water. There are all kinds of things moving about, and flood waters are always a bit contaminated."

"No worries there," she said as she watched the snake move on to the next tree.

"Better get busy, then," he said. "We need to get back to the farm soon. It won't be long until everyone shows up for supper."

Being at the farm with Gabe and helping the ladies with the food efforts had been a gratifying experience for Kennedy. She had gotten to know so many of her neighbors, and there was a closeness she felt among members of the little community that was heartwarming and reassuring. Gabe had been right; these were strong people, and as she watched him lead them out of this crisis and how they held each other up, she realized how lucky she was to have found this place.

The little guest cottage at the farm was comfortable, and though built to match the farmhouse, it had a charm all its own. While she was glad to have the comfort and privacy of the cottage, she felt a little guilty as she watched the other members of the community camp out nightly in the farmhouse rooms, spreading out and finding little areas to make their own. They were all grateful, though, for the creature comforts of air conditioning and fresh water as the power outage stretched into nearly a week with no end in sight. Several, who could get to their homes through the flooded roads, had gone home and were making do, but the elderly and those with infants and small children had stayed.

Every night, after the house had settled down, Gabe would come to the cottage to see her. They would sit and share a drink or a glass of wine and talk about the day and the happenings around the community. With each passing day, the community recovered a little more and got closer to getting back on its feet, but they still had a long way to go. They all prayed that the power trucks would soon roll through the neighborhood, a sign that life as they knew it would soon resume.

"Gabe, you look exhausted," she said as she handed him a glass of wine. "How much longer do you think it will be before we get some outside help in here?"

"I talked to a buddy of mine at the power company today, and he said he hoped they would get out here in the next day or two. The whole county is pretty torn up, and they're spread pretty thin.

He said his guys have been working around the clock, but it's slow going."

"It will be such a relief to get power back. I know these people are anxious to get back to their homes," she said. "How's it going with getting the roads cleaned up?"

"Not bad, aside from some of the flooded roads, mostly everything is passable now. We've been piling up the debris in several central areas and getting it ready to burn. Everything's still wet, so that may be a while."

As he talked, she noticed the numerous scratches, cuts, and bruises on his hands and forearms. He had been working nonstop for the better part of the week, and the toll it was taking on him was showing. She wondered how long he and the other men could keep up the pace. Adsila and the ladies provided breakfast and supper daily for the community and kept things going without complaint. It was a monumental effort, and she was continually in awe of these people's tenacity and resolve. That night, before she went to sleep, she prayed for God to give strength to the little community and the people in it so they could persevere and endure for as long as it took to get the Oasis back on her feet.

The following day word spread through the community that someone had seen power trucks working up near the main road. The news lifted everyone's spirits, and a renewed energy among the working men and women was palpable. As Kennedy helped the women prepare the food for the evening meal, she noticed that even Adsila, who had never once lost her cheery disposition throughout the ordeal, seemed refreshed and replenished as she hummed while she cut vegetables and laughed with the other ladies.

When Gabe stopped in at the farm in the early afternoon, he said the power trucks were in the neighborhood's interior now, and

136

a South Carolina crew had come in to help. At nearly every crossroads in the Oasis, men were working hard to restore power to the community. It would not be long now.

That evening, as Kennedy and Gabe shared their wine, there was a brief second when the power from the generators waned and switched over, and power was restored to the farm. Kennedy didn't understand what was happening at first, but she knew when she saw Gabe's broad smile. They hugged each other in celebration and then went to the big house to spread the news. As if by clockwork, the inhabitants had started gathering up their things as they were anxious to return to their homes and start living their everyday lives again. Within the hour, almost everyone had gone except for a few who were waiting until morning.

Kennedy went back to the guesthouse and gathered her things, wanting to get back to her little cabin, settle in and make sure everything was ok. When Gabe came over from the farmhouse and saw her packing, he felt melancholy at the prospect of her leaving. Having her at the farm these past days had been comforting and seeing her every night had helped him keep going. Now that she was leaving, the farm would become a lonely place for him again.

"You don't have to go tonight," he said. "You could stay one more night, and I'll take you home in the morning,"

"I know; I'm just anxious to check on the place and make sure everything is ok," she said with a smile, feeling his sadness as he watched her pack. "I'll come back in the morning and help you clean things up here on the farm. There's a lot to do to get your house back the way it was," she said with a chuckle.

"Oh," he said, "don't worry about that. I've got a little lady that cleans for me. She comes twice a week, but there is never much for her to do since it's just me here. But she needs the money, so I have her come all the same. She will be grateful for the extra days and to have more to do."

Kennedy smiled. So many people depended on this man's kindness.

"I could take you down tonight," he continued, "and we could check on things and start getting the place cooled down. It's been sitting for a while now, so it will take a while. Then you could come back here to sleep and go home in the morning."

She realized he was lobbying hard for her to stay, and her heart constricted a little thinking about how lonely it must be here for him at the farm by himself all of the time.

"Ok, that sounds good," she said as she set her bag down. She saw his face visibly soften, and she was glad she hadn't been stubborn about going home. Besides, they both needed a little downtime from the stress of the last week. Having a quiet evening on the farm would do them both some good.

Driving through the narrow roads of the Oasis, Kennedy was amazed at all the work the men had done since she'd seen it a few days ago. The roads were mostly cleared and groomed, and, aside from the huge piles of tree limbs and debris here and there, the neighborhood looked good. It was heartwarming to see the lights of the homes glowing through the trees as the little community's inhabitants returned to the business of living normally.

As they pulled down the driveway and Gabe's truck lights lit up the back of the cabin, Kennedy suddenly had a heart full of pride for her little place. The old cabin had stood strong in the storm, and the place was no worse for the wear. She noticed Gabe had fixed the tin that had peeled back on the porch roof, and aside from the bare porches, it looked the same as it had before the storm. Looking back over the week, she realized it had been a turning point. She knew now, without hesitation or reservation, that she belonged there.

Chapter Ten

"For there is nothing hidden that will not be disclosed, and nothing concealed that will not be known or brought out into the open." Luke 8:17

Slowly over the next couple of weeks, things returned to normal in the Oasis. Though a reminder of their hardships, the smoldering piles of debris also served as an encouraging sign that the hurricane and its aftermath would only be a memory soon. Kennedy knew that with the storm had come a new day for her. Though she was still not sleeping well, she felt more hope than she had since fleeing Miami after the deaths of her family. Maybe she could build a new life here after all.

Memories of the persistent dreams plagued her, and she took a couple of hours each morning to shake off the effects. It wasn't until she saw the first light in the eastern sky she felt peace again. It was one reason she loved the sunrises on her front porch. The rising sun always brought with it a new hope.

She also remembered that the historical records office would likely be open again with the new month. The thought of meeting Miss Olivia and learning more about her cabin and the Oasis was a welcome distraction, and she had decided to, once again, make the trip to the old courthouse to see what she could discover. Gabe had needed to turn his attention to the orders piling up at the sawmill, especially since the hurricane, for the next few days, so it would be a good time for her to make the trip and spend the afternoon with Miss Olivia.

As she drove along the back roads, she felt saddened by the sights of the old granddaddy oaks, and ancient pines in the pastures brought down by the hurricane. It seemed the effects of Hurricane Alene had been felt far and wide. Many of the rural houses had tarps on their roofs and barns damaged. These people didn't get on the national news, and no resources were rushing in to help them.

The old courthouse with its high clocks tower was a welcome sight as Kennedy pulled into a spot on the side of the building. She was still fascinated by the place and wanted to learn more about its history. The man at the receiving desk remembered her immediately and again pointed down the hallway to the right. She nodded and smiled as she breezed past him on her way to the little office at the end of the hall. Her heart leapt when she saw the old door with its hand-painted frosted glass and antique crystal doorknob. She was hopeful she could finally satisfy some of her curiosity about her little cabin and the little river community she had come to love. She tapped lightly on the glass, opened the door slowly, and poked her head inside. When she saw no one, she called out to see if anyone was in the office.

Olivia Lafayette was nothing like Kennedy had imagined. She had pictured a frail, little old lady with tiny wire-rimmed glasses perched on her nose, but Miss Olivia was anything but. As she came booming out of a side room, albeit with her cane, she was the picture of spryness and in charge of all of her faculties. She enthusiastically greeted Kennedy, clearly excited someone had come to see her. Kennedy guessed she didn't get too many visitors.

"Hello there!" she yelled from across the room.

"Hi!" Kennedy answered with a smile. "I've come to find out some information and history on a property I've just bought here in the county. Have I come to the right place?"

"You sure have," she said with a laugh. "If there's anything to know about it, you'll find it here. What's your name, sugar?"

"I'm Kennedy Klark," she said. "You must be Miss Olivia?"

"Why yes, I am," she said in a Southern accent with a distinct sophistication. Kennedy guessed her personal history in the county was a long one.

"Wonderful, I've heard you know everything there is to know about our little county. Where's the best place to start if I want to research my property?" Kennedy said as she looked around at the old cabinets and library shelves. The place smelled of old papers and books, and the feeling of history there was palpable.

"Well, with me, of course," Olivia said, pointing to the beautifully carved table in the middle of the room. "Have a seat and tell me about this property of yours."

As Kennedy told her about her property, she saw Olivia's eyes light up in recognition. The more Kennedy told her what she was hoping to learn about the property and the neighborhood, the more excited Olivia became. Kennedy could tell this would be a fruitful and exciting visit.

"You certainly do have an interesting property and one of the oldest houses in the county," she said as she got up and went to one of the old cabinets. She pulled out a set of rolled-up maps and brought them to the table, where the two women spread them out.

"This," Olivia said as she pointed to an area on the map, "is the area where the Oasis sits now. But, back in the day, the pioneer family that settled there owned it all, including some of the property on the other side of the river. They grew cotton, tobacco, and a handful of other crops on the high ground out of the floodplain. They used the rest to raise livestock. The proximity to the river was ideal because they could ferry their crops to market more quickly than they could over the rough roads. We don't have much history of the family before they settled here in this office, other than they had traveled down from the Northeast through the Carolinas and

142

Georgia. You can probably learn more about them through other historical resources. We know they had several children but only have a little in the way of birth records. We know the property sat relatively dormant for a while, and then there was a bit of a squabble as to what to do with it among the descendants, some wanting to sell and some wanting to keep it. That's how the little cabin you came to own got carved away from the original homestead. Among the heirs, it was a compromise to keep the cabin and the 25 acres it sat on and sell the remaining land to the man who eventually developed the Oasis. By the way, the man who developed the property was so enthralled by its beauty when he first saw it that he told his partner it was like an Oasis, and the name stuck. Right here is an area within the large tract of land the family wanted to set aside as common space for the community. It's a piece of land where an old tobacco barn sits, and I think the folks who live there use it as a community center and church. They wished to preserve the land and the building, which was part of the original farm."

"Yes," Kennedy said. "I know it. It's called the Pavilion."

"That's right," Olivia said. "And that old barn sits on about 50 acres of prime, old hardwood forest. Many a lawyer has tried to figure out how to break up that trust, but it's airtight," she said with a chuckle.

"Now about your cabin…" she began." We think it was built in the early 1900s, though the records about it are scarce. We don't think it was the original home built by the pioneers, a structure that was that old in the woods would be long gone by now. We began to see references to the family in other documents around 1860, which would make sense. The cabin has never been added to the national registry of historical places, though it should be. No one has ever seemed to take much interest in it until now. Eventually, the heirs did decide to sell it, though, to a man named Willer, I think, in the

143

early 1990s. There are some birth, death, and marriage records over there that you can comb through," she said as she pointed to one of the cabinets, "as well as some deed and title records if you want to look for more. If you need some help, I'll be over here in the side office, so just holler at me."

"How will I know what to look for?" Kennedy asked. "Where do I start?"

"Well, my dear, you will need a name," she said as her eyes sparkled. " The original homestead family was a large Irish Catholic family by the name of O'Brien."

Kennedy tried to hide her surprise at recognizing her mother's maiden name, which her mother gave to her as her middle name. The chances of the O'Briens who settled the homestead being related to her mother's side of the family were remote. It added a little mystery and intrigue, though, that motivated her even more as she dug into the records.

She looked through the property and title records first. Being an attorney, she felt she could decipher them easily and understand the transactions' nuances. When she found the deed that conveyed the property from the original O'Brien family to the developer, she scanned the list of names of grantors, looking for anything familiar. One grantor was Liam Michael O'Brien, who shared a first name with her brother. Kennedy knew that Liam was a common Irish name and that the chances this Liam was related to her were probably slim to none. Having no living grandparents, she had no one to ask if she wanted to know more. She knew little about her mother's side of the family, and with both her parents being only children, their family history was scant. Still, she felt compelled to ask Olivia if she could make a copy so she could research it further if she wanted. This same name also appeared in the records when the family sold the cabin and surrounding land into a trust, which she assumed must have had a connection to the man named Willer.

Next, she looked through the records of birth, death, and marriages. The O'Brien family's records covered a short period starting in the late 1860s and included only one child of the original O'Brien settlers. Kennedy assumed it was likely because the other children had been born elsewhere before they arrived in the little county. As she looked further, she was sad to see a death record for this child at nine and wondered what had happened but could find no more information about it. Kennedy realized that many of these records were drawn from the entries of family bibles and the residents' memories, as there were no public records so they were likely to be incomplete. Anything in the historical records office was painstakingly collected, organized, and cataloged by its volunteers. To her disappointment, the O'Brien family records quickly dwindled as she assumed that the children and subsequent grandchildren moved on from the county to make their homes elsewhere in the state and beyond. With little else there of interest about the family, she perused the other records a little to see what else she could discover. She came upon a list of families that had been longtime residents of the county and scanned it for any recognition. When her eyes landed on the name Barrett, she thought it would be interesting to look up the history of Gabe's family and the old farm.

From the records, she saw that Gabe's great-grandfather purchased the land on which the farm sat in the early 1900s. It consisted of over 200 acres, much more acreage than Kennedy realized. It was not, she was surprised to find, formally part of the Oasis, though it shared a long border with the community on its eastern side. It had been passed through the generations to the subsequent heirs and eventually solely to Gabe about ten years prior. She knew he had a sister and wondered how that had transpired but assumed Gabe had purchased her interest when his parents had passed away but could find no record of the transaction. Searching a little further, she found his birth record showing he had been born on August 19, 1982, to Henry Lee Barrett and Sara Jane Wilcox Barrett, at 9:57 am at their home on the farm. She thought this to be a little unusual as Sara, at 44, would have likely been advised to deliver in a hospital in case of complications. When she scanned the rest of the birth record, she saw that an attending physician, Dr. A. B. Lafayette, had signed it. She also found a copy of the Barrett family bible showing the births, deaths, and marriages through the years though the entries had ended with the marriage of Gabe's parents, or so she thought until she looked at the last page. There she saw an addendum entry, obviously added after the original bible had been copied and entered into the records. It had only one entry:

Birth: Gabriel Alexander Barrett, born to Sara Lee Barrett,

August 19, 1982

Kennedy puzzled over the entry and wondered who had added it to the records. Aside from someone having added later, whoever had done the entry had gotten the names mixed up. She decided to point out the error to Olivia so she could correct the entry knowing she was meticulous about accuracy.

"Miss Olivia," she called out, "may I show you something I found?"

"Certainly," she said as she came and sat down again with Kennedy at the table.

"I believe there's an error here," Kennedy said as she handed her the copy of the entry. "According to the birth record, the mother's name was Sara Jane Barrett, not Sara Lee Barrett. It looks like someone got the names mixed up."

Olivia visibly paled and tried to speak, opening her mouth and then shutting it tight. Kennedy was confused as to why the older woman would have had such a visceral reaction to what she had shown her. A long moment passed. Olivia covered her face with both hands and then slowly let her hands slide down from her face to rest on the table, one on top of the other. She let out a deep sigh and looked Kennedy straight in the eye.

"I'm afraid I've been found out," she said quietly as her face contorted in near tears. "I thought it would go unnoticed in the records for many years to come. Long enough so that no one would ever be hurt by it." She paused, then took a deep, shaky breath and continued. "It's not a mistake. I'm the one who made the additional birth entry. My husband was the family physician of the Barretts for many years. When their daughter Sara Lee was just 14 years old, she became pregnant. Her mother discovered the pregnancy when she accidentally walked into Sara's room while she was dressing. The girl was nearly six months along and was barely showing, but just enough for her mother to be able to tell. The Barretts called my husband and asked him to come to the house to examine Sara and help them decide what to do. There, the three of them came up with a plan to pretend that it was Sara Jane, not Sara Lee, who was pregnant. They agreed my husband would deliver the baby at home and sign the baby's birth records as the child of Henry and Sara Jane to protect Sara Lee from the shame of being an unwed mother. Besides, at 14, they felt she could not care for the baby. Everyone thought it was the right thing to do at the time. The plan went off without a hitch, and the boy, Gabriel, was raised as their son, no one ever being the wiser. Through the years, up until he passed, it always bothered my husband. He knew it had saved a lot of heartache at the time, but he always felt the boy deserved to know the truth but Henry and Sara never got around to telling him. Sara Lee was never the same afterward. I think she was bitter about the whole thing, left for college, and has never come home. After Henry and Sara passed and my husband as well, I decided to add the birth record. I just felt that somewhere, the truth needed to be recorded. I never thought it would be discovered while the boy was still alive." She stopped to catch her breath. "Kennedy," she said, "may I ask, do you have any intentions of doing anything with this information?"

Kennedy was so shocked she couldn't answer. That she held in her hands the only document that proved who Gabe's mother really was unreal to her. Of all the people in the world to discover the truth, she could not believe it was her. Had it not been for divine intervention, she believed it would have been hidden forever, or at least until no one would have cared about it. She had no idea what she should or shouldn't do with the information. She finally looked at Olivia, saw how distraught the older woman looked, and felt sad for her. *Good intentions*, she thought, *are often the seedlings of the things in life that hurt us the most.*

Sara Lee sat on her patio, enjoying the warm weather of summer in the suburbs of Toronto. Since moving there ten years prior, she had tried to soak up as many of the sun's rays as possible to ward off the gloom she felt during the long winter months. Having grown up in Florida, she was aware that even after all these years, her body still craved the vital effects the sunshine would provide. Her issues with depression through the years had been significant, and her doctors had attributed much of it to seasonal affective disorder, but she knew it was more than that. It had started soon after Gabe was born.

To say having a baby at 14 was traumatic was an understatement, but for Sara, the real trauma had begun after. She'd had him in late August and was back in school with her friends right after Labor Day. She'd had almost no time to process and recover from the pregnancy and birth, either physically or emotionally. Her parents had told friends and family she was away at camp all summer when she had really been hidden away in the farmhouse with nothing to do and only her shame to keep her company. She had not even known she was pregnant until her mother spotted her slightly round tummy when she'd mistakenly walked into Sara's bedroom while she was dressing. She had felt her body changing over time, but she was too naive to understand what was happening to her. The same could be said for the cool fall evening she had conceived Gabe.

He'd been visiting his cousins at their cabin in the Oasis for the Thanksgiving holiday. All the kids in the neighborhood had been hanging out together on the river and at the springs, enjoying the break from school. He was older than she, turning 17 the month before, and with his tall, sturdy frame and light blue eyes, his gaze had turned her knees to jelly whenever he looked at her. All the kids would sit around the bonfire in the woods at night, tell ghost stories, and make s'mores. Some of the older kids would bring beer, and on one night, he opened one and handed it to her. Not wanting to look stupid and having no experience with alcohol, she took it from him and drank it down more quickly than she should have. Before she felt its effects, he placed another in her hand. Later, he took her by the hand and led her through the woods to one of the little bunkhouses his aunt and uncle built on their property. He assured her he was the only one staying there and no one would come in or disturb them. By the light of a candle, he had gently and sweetly taken her virginity and sealed his place in her heart forever as her first love. The night before he left, he'd taken her to the bunkhouse one more time, and she cried when he told her he would go home the next day. They promised to write, but they never had.

She knew almost nothing about the conception of babies or the process of pregnancy, so when her body changed several months later, she had no idea why. It wasn't until Dr. Lafayette had come to the house and carefully examined her that she understood what was happening to her. When her mother explained what they would do, she was too shocked and ashamed even to question it.

149

When Gabe was born, the birth was excruciating and terrifying. No one had prepared her for what she would experience, and being at home in her bed, with no idea how long it would last, had overwhelmed and broken her. Dr. Lafayette had done his best to guide her through, but without the tools available to him in a hospital to alleviate her pain, he could not do much to help her.

After Gabe arrived, her mother had whisked him away, and she'd barely been able to lay eyes on him. Over the next few days, as she recovered from the birth, she could hear him crying in the next room, and something inside tugged at her. When she had asked to see him, her mother had told her not to worry about him, he was doing fine in her care, and she could see him when she felt better. By the time Sara was up and around, Gabe was completely under her mother's charge. When he cried, she fed him or changed him. When it was time for him to sleep, he was tucked away in a bassinet next to her mother's bed, and before Sara knew it, she was back in school, and that she'd ever been pregnant or had a baby had been swept completely under the rug.

As time went by, it became easier and easier to accept the charade that the family was living. Gabe felt much like a little brother to her rather than her son. As she got older, she became more and more detached from her motherly instincts, and it was natural he spent more time with her mother than with her. But as the years went by, she also understood better and examined her mother's motives.

Sara Jane had experienced a difficult time conceiving. It had taken years of trying before she had become pregnant with Sara Lee, and after she was born, she'd had little hope of ever conceiving another child. They tried for a few years but finally gave up and accepted that Sara Lee would be their only child. When she discovered that Sara Lee was pregnant, raising Gabe as her own came to her immediately. To her, it was the perfect solution to an exceedingly difficult situation. When she had approached Henry with the idea, he had expressed reservations, but upon her insistence, he saw the merit in considering it. Sara Lee could go on with her life, reputation intact, and Sara Jane could raise another child, fulfilling what he suspected was a deep, dark hole in her soul. When Dr. Lafayette had agreed to help them with the plan, he felt like maybe it was meant to be.

Sara Jane knew that she could not let Sara Lee bond with the child. Doing so would endanger the entire plan and could cause Sara Lee to buck the idea and insist that she raise the child as her son. She knew in her heart of hearts she was acting in her self-interest, but her outward stance was that it was what was best for Gabe and Sara Lee. The longer the situation went on, and with the birth certificate issued, she knew it would become harder and harder to reverse course.

But as Sara Lee got older, her resentment toward her parents, particularly her mother, grew. When she left for college, Gabe was only 4 years old. She used to dream about going back for him, and in her dreams, it was a happy, joyful reunion. But in the light of day, she realized that he was a little boy who had what he believed to be, a mommy and daddy who loved him and who he also loved dearly. She could not complain about his care as they doted on the boy and afforded him every advantage. Her father was kind and attentive and had much time to devote to raising Gabe in the rich and wholesome environment on the farm and at the river. Her mother could not have shown the boy more love. So as much as she felt the urge to right the situation, she could never imagine a good outcome for any of them, especially Gabe. As time passed, returning became harder and harder. She realized that having left home for college when Gabe was so young meant he likely had little memory of her and that it was probably better to keep it that way. Going home meant opening up old wounds.

When she married and had more children, the magnitude of what her mother had done had descended on her in ways she could not comprehend. When her sons were born, their cries would take her back to those first few days in the farmhouse after Gabe was born, and she would struggle with what everyone believed was postpartum depression, but she knew better. As the two boys grew, she would constantly compare them to her memories of him, and as they became young adults, she imagined that was what Gabe looked like long after she'd been home for the last time.

She did, now and then, peek into his life to experience a little of it and to see what kind of man he had grown into. She was in the auditorium when he graduated from college and behind a chain-linked fence in her car when he returned from his last deployment overseas, the sight of him in his Navy uniform bringing her to proud tears. When he received the Medal of Honor, she watched on C-span as the President of the United States placed the medal around his neck. Her mother had been too ill to attend the ceremony, and her father could not leave her, so Gabe had accepted his medal alone, save for a family friend of her father's who she barely remembered. Her regrets were long and had she had the chance to do it all over again, things would have been different.

When her parents passed, so close to one another, she had let him bear that burden alone and had not gone home for their funerals. She couldn't make herself go as much as she knew it was wrong. Seeing him would have been too difficult, and she had emotionally separated from her parents long ago. She knew that soon she would add that to her list of regrets too. She had given him exactly nothing in his 28 years, not even her love and attention, so when he contacted her about the farm and her half of the inheritance, she knew what she wanted to do. Though it was a sizable estate containing many valuable assets, the farm being only one of them, she had, without hesitation, signed everything over to him. At least it gave her a little solace; she could give him something even if she knew he perceived it not as a gift but as indifference. Ten years later, she shuddered at what he must think of her now.

Chapter Eleven

"I have told you these things, so that in me you may have peace. In this world, you will have trouble. But take heart! I have overcome the world." John 16:33

Kennedy was deep in thought as she drove her Jeep along the rural roads back to the Oasis, her heart saddened by the weight of the knowledge thrust upon her. She had no idea what she would do about what she had learned. To do nothing with it felt wrong, but she couldn't imagine how she could ever tell him. Parts of his soul were already fragile and shaking his entire foundation and sense of who he was would be cruel and potentially disastrous. There was no clear, right path, she realized. It was a terrible dilemma. There was only one person in the world she knew she could talk to about this but even doing that seemed dangerous. Talking about a secret could sometimes make it take on a life of its own.

She felt tired and drained. The dreams descended upon her nearly every night. She would awaken around 3:00 am, sometimes in a cold sweat but always frightened. Each time the disconnected dreams about her family and the accident jolted her out of sleep. She could never remember them clearly or tie the pieces of the dreams together.

She would toss and turn and try to go back to sleep, but most times, she would get up and sit in the big chair by the fireplace, helpless to rid herself of the thoughts of her entire family perishing in the inferno of the doomed boat. Lately, at the end of her rope, with her inability to sleep through the night, she had prayed to help

153

her get back to sleep. She'd had, for a while, a nagging feeling that the dreams were trying to push her toward something, but she had no idea what that was. Sometimes, God would grant her some mercy, and she could fall back into a peaceful sleep for a couple of hours. When the sun rose, she would usually feel a reprieve from the disturbing thoughts and feelings, though it was getting harder and harder to shake them.

She tapped lightly on Finn's screen door and heard him beckon her in from somewhere in the back of the house. When he saw her, he seemed to recognize that something was amiss. Once they settled into the rockers on the back porch, he wasted no time trying to get to the bottom of whatever it was.

"What's bothering you, Kenny?" he asked. She had never been more grateful for his forthright nature. All the way to his cabin, she'd been struggling to come up with a way to bring up the subject. She sighed a little and set her gaze on the foraging chickens in the backyard of the little homestead.

"Finn," she asked, "what do you know about Gabe's childhood?" She saw him visibly stiffen, and the question hung heavily in the air for a minute. He shifted in his seat and turned to look at her.

"I think the question here, Kenny, is what is it that you know?" he said and waited, giving her no wiggle room to evade his question.

"I went to the courthouse today to do a little research on my cabin and the origins of the Oasis, and I-ah stumbled onto some information. Now, I don't know what I'm supposed to do about it," she said.

"Well," he said. "That makes two of us. I've struggled with this for a lot of years. But, for the life of me, I've never been able to see

154

where any good would come from telling him, especially now." He sighed and paused a minute, then went on," I've seen a change in him since you got here, Kenny, a good change. I'm starting to see glimpses of the boy I knew before he went off to war, and I'd hate to see anything get in the way of that. I'm of the opinion that, if he were ever to be told, there is only one person on this earth who should do the telling. And it isn't you or me."

Kennedy thought about that for a minute, then nodded. Finn was right. It was not her place to tell him, at least not now.

"I think you are right about that, Finn," she said as she turned to look at him." Do you think it will ever happen? Do you think she will ever come back here?"

"I just don't know, Kenny," he said with a long sigh. "But what I do know is that sometimes secrets aren't meant to be told. Sometimes it's better to let sleeping dogs lie."

———————

Kennedy was restless back at the cabin, and she was thankful Gabe was busy at the sawmill. She was sure that if he laid eyes on her, he would know something wasn't right and press her for details. As tired as her mind was, she wasn't sure she could think fast enough to come up with something to throw him off course.

She'd only had a few hours of sleep the night before, and with nothing in front of her she had to do, she thought she might lie down for a while, maybe catch a nap before dinner to take the edge off her fatigue. She stretched out on the bed, grabbed the afghan she'd draped across the end to cover her, and closed her eyes. In only seconds sleep had overcome her, and in her mind's eye, she saw images, clear and bright this time, as though she were watching a movie.

The 84-foot Viking yacht, the Not Guilty, was nestled majestically in her moorings, her lights ablaze, indicating that she was ready to go to sea. She saw her parents and her brother onboard and asleep in their staterooms. Suddenly, she saw smoke so thick it enveloped them, and they disappeared into an impenetrable haze. She could hear them gasping for air, and as the fire engulfed the boat in a rage, she saw men in dark clothing running, leaving the yacht. They moved quickly but quietly and disappeared into the night. Next, she saw the boat in smoldering ruins as the morning sky lightened with the dawn and an osprey perched on the mast of a nearby sailing yacht. Suddenly he turned to look at her and left his high lookout flying directly toward her. As he neared her, his wingspan threatened to engulf her, his piercing eyes bore into her, and instantly the scene went black.

Kennedy's eyes flew open. She took a minute to orient herself as the images were still fresh and raw in her mind. When she could slow her breathing and ground herself, she went back through the painful scenes in her mind, remembering them in exquisite detail. This dream had been different. The sights, sounds, and smells of the dream had been vivid, not disconnected and vague like the dreams before.

Feeling unnerved, she could lay there no longer. She got out of bed, turned on the reading light, and sat at the antique writing desk. She found a pen and pad and wrote down the details of what she had seen in the dream, trying to capture as much detail as possible. As she wrote, she realized what the dreams had been about. She now knew that her heart, from the beginning, had felt it had not been an accident. The images of the men leaving the boat in her dream had confirmed that for her. Now she was left with the idea her family had died at the hands of men and not from some horrific accident. The visions propelled her out of the fog of grief that had shrouded her thinking for the last couple of months. She had been jolted into the cold reality that there were dark possibilities surrounding this tragedy.

She was resolute now in finding the answers to these ominous questions. How did this happen? Why would anyone want to harm her family if it was not an accident? She hadn't been on the yacht because of an emergency at work, and she had canceled her plans last minute to join them. She wondered if survivor's guilt was driving this.

Had she been there, could she have saved them? Did they suffer? Did they know they were dying? The thought of the torment and the pain of them burning to death was unbearable and inconceivable. She hadn't allowed herself to think of these questions before, but now, with the dreams becoming clearer, she was forced to contemplate them. There were questions she needed answers to if she would ever heal from this tragedy.

There were things about the tragedy that had bothered her from the beginning. Her father had been meticulous about everything, but with his boats, that was an understatement. This particular boat, the *Not Guilty*, had been the boat he had dreamed of owning his entire adult life. He had spent years researching this yacht and the exact specifications of the boat he would one day buy. He had always owned beautiful boats, but this one was special. This yacht represented to him the achievement of his lifelong goals and meeting his personal expectations of success. The day he brought the *Not Guilty* to the Yacht Club, and put her in her slip, had been one of the happiest days of his life.

As meticulous as he was about the details of the yacht and its appointments, nothing compared to his attention to safety. He had outfitted every boat he'd ever owned with the best equipment, and the *Not Guilty* had been no exception. Fire was always one of the highest threats, especially at sea, so he always invested in the latest and most state-of-the-art fire suppression systems. Money was no object for protecting the lives of his family while they were in his care aboard his boat. That fire had destroyed the yacht and taken the lives of everyone on board seemed unbelievable to her.

Unable to clear her mind of the visions and the questions the dreams had brought, she took a walk. The day had cooled down with the arrival of an afternoon rainstorm, and it still had a couple of hours before the sun would set. As she walked along the tree-shaded lanes, she felt her mind calm. She heard the birds busying themselves before nightfall and the cicadas winding down their relentless drone. She felt grateful for the peace and serenity the Oasis offered, not able to imagine how she would have coped with all this if she were still in Miami.

Up ahead, she saw the Pavilion, the old barn looking sublime in the early evening light. She visited it, and when she stepped inside, she immediately felt the reverence of the place. Though it was nothing like the churches she had grown up in, she felt closer to God here than in any other place of worship. She sat down on the worn wooden floor in the shadow of the old cross and prayed to God for strength, guidance, and clarity. With everything seemingly revealed to her that day, she felt these were what she needed the most. Lost in her thoughts, she did not hear the footsteps coming behind her.

"Kennedy?" Adsila asked in a soft voice. "Are you ok?"

"Oh, Adsila, yes, I'm ok," she said as she looked up," just a really tough day, that's all."

Adsila extended her hand to Kennedy and helped her up off the floor. "Let's go over here where we can sit for a moment together and talk." The two women found a couple of chairs, sat down, and were quiet for a minute. "Now tell me, Kennedy," she said, taking both her hands in her own. "What's going on?"

Kennedy sighed and looked up, not knowing where to begin. "It's the dreams, " she said, finally, and paused for a moment." Ever since I got here, I've had these really frightening and disturbing dreams. I don't know if Gabe has told you about what happened to my family and me."

"He did," she said. "But only in confidence and out of concern for you. He wanted some advice on how he could best help you."

"It's ok; I'm not upset about him telling you. It's been a relief to talk about it." She took a deep, ragged breath. "The dreams I've been having are about the tragedy. They were vague and confusing for a while, and I couldn't make any sense of them. But the last one was very vivid, and the images I saw were clear and very disturbing. I saw the boat and the fire, my parents dying," she paused as her voice caught in her throat. Adsila squeezed her hand to encourage her to go on. "I also saw two men running from the boat after the flames engulfed it. And then there was the osprey."

"Osprey?" Adsila said.

"Yes, there was an osprey in the dream who flew at me with a compelling look in his eye, sort of like he was warning me or sending me a message. I don't know; it's probably because I've had an osprey hanging around my property since I got here."

Adsila looked her straight in the eye, paused, and took a deep breath. "Kennedy, you know I have a deep Christian faith, but my Cherokee ancestors firmly believed seeing the osprey, whether in a dream or real life, was symbolic of a mystical and often important message." After a long pause, Adsila said, "I didn't know how to tell you this, but I have also seen an osprey in my dreams. In my dreams, he is speaking to you. I didn't know what to make of it, but now I do."

Kennedy didn't know how to absorb all that had been revealed to her that day. She needed time to digest everything and time to think things through. Thankfully, with its quiet tranquility, the Oasis and the river were a good place to sort things out and figure out a plan to get to the truth. Whatever that may be, she knew she would not heal until she did.

She'd left Miami shortly after losing her parents and brother. Being in the city where she'd grown up with them was just too painful. Even though she had been in shock and grief-stricken, the whole thing still seemed unreal to her. She had survived the first few days by going through the motions as if she were outside herself, watching it happen to someone else. Looking back, she realized she had been in sheer survival mode to keep herself sane and functioning. There had been no one to help her, no one to plan the funerals, and no one to guide her through the many important decisions she'd had to make. It's no wonder to her now that she had fled.

When she'd found the little cabin online, it had struck a strong chord with her. She'd called the real estate office handling the sale and made a full-price, cash offer with no contingencies. Ten days later, she was on her way to North Florida, knowing almost nothing about her destination. Once she made it to the Oasis, away from news reports and constant reminders, she could function again somewhat. Now that she'd had time to pull herself together and start her new life, it was time to get answers.

The law enforcement agency's investigation began the morning after the tragedy while the fire was still smoldering. Because the deaths had occurred on the water, many agencies were involved. Because a fire was involved, it became even more complicated. Arson was a real possibility, so fire investigators worked to determine where the fire had originated within the vessel. They had worked alongside detectives, crime scene technicians from the local police department, and other officials working on the case.

The law enforcement officials and other agencies had not released information to the press or the public. It was a sensitive case and one considered a high priority. On the surface, the investigation had revealed nothing out of the ordinary. The Klarks, by all appearances, seemed to be a happy family. Keegan Klark had a lucrative law practice, and his son, Liam, practiced with him. From interviewing the employees, they found they had a strong working relationship and made an excellent and powerful legal team. There seemed to be no marital issues between Keegan Klark and his wife, and the investigation revealed no affairs. There was absolutely nothing that pointed to any foul play. They determined that Kennedy, who practiced at another law firm, had shared a close relationship with both her parents and her brother.

They interviewed her immediately, asking about her whereabouts and why she had not been on the boat with her family as planned. They ceased questioning her when it became apparent that she offered nothing of real substance. Though Kennedy would inherit the family fortune and was also the sole beneficiary of several large life insurance policies, they assured her she was not a person of interest in the deaths. But she still felt like no one trusted her completely. With her loss, that feeling was too much for her to endure.

Due to her father's notoriety in the legal community, her family's deaths dominated the news. He had recently won several significant cases and had been prominent even in the national news. Teams from news agencies descended on the scene immediately and sought her out for interviews night and day. News persons passed through security at her condo, hoping to get a glimpse or corner her with questions. As soon as she was able, she left Miami.

Adsila took Kennedy back to her cabin in her side-by-side as night was falling over the Oasis. She hugged her and encouraged her to pursue her instincts, if for no other reason than to put the matter to rest.

"I'm truly sorry about the loss of your family Kennedy," she'd said as she hugged her goodbye. "I can't imagine what you've been through. But please know that I am here for you, day or night, whenever you need me. Promise me you'll call if I can help?"

"Thank you, Adsila, that means the world to me. And, I will, I promise. Thank you for listening. It helped me sort out what I want to do."

"You're welcome, my dear friend. Tomorrow, then?"

"Yes," Kennedy said with a smile, "tomorrow."

After Adsila dropped her off, she prepared a simple dinner of roast chicken, rice, and vegetables. She needed something hearty and comforting after realizing she had not had a bite to eat all day. She was pulling it out of the oven when there was a knock at her door, and when she peeked out the kitchen window, she saw Gabe's truck in the driveway.

"Oh," she said, as she opened the door, "you're just in time."

"Really? Just in time for what?"

"Dinner," she said. "I've just taken it out of the oven."

"Oh, well, ok, that's not why I'm here, but I am hungry," he said with a laugh.

"Can I make you a drink?"

"Why don't you let me do that?" he said. "Can dinner wait a few minutes? It would be great if we could just sit together for a bit."

"Sure," she said. "Of course."

Gabe poured a couple of bourbons over ice, and they sat together on the couch, each settling in for a moment, not talking.

"How are things?" he finally asked as he turned to her. "I haven't seen you for a couple of days."

"Ok," she said. "I've been busy sorting out some things. Today I went to the courthouse and found some history of the cabin and the Oasis."

"Really?" he said. "Tell me what you found out?"

"Well," she said. "You were right. The pioneer family built the cabin in the early 1900s though it was probably not the original structure here. The family owned a whole bunch of land here where the Oasis sits and some across the river too. The most interesting thing I found out was that the pioneer family's name was O'Brien. That was my mother's maiden name. It's also my middle name."

"Really?" he said. "That is interesting. Do you think they are related to you?"

"Oh, I don't know," she said, "a lot of Irish families settled here in Florida, and O'Brien is a pretty common Irish name. Worth checking out, though, I guess."

They both contemplated that as they sipped their drink

"So what else?" he said as he studied her face.

"What," she asked, "what do you mean?"

"What else have you been sorting out?" he said, his light blue eyes searching hers.

She looked at him for a minute, then sighed. "I guess you know that ever since I got here, I've been having trouble sleeping," she said. He nodded, then let her go on. "It's mainly because of the dreams, the nightmares; I've been dreaming about the fire and the deaths of my family," she said. She was struggling, but he didn't interrupt. "For a while, it was just fragments, scattered images, but now the dreams have become vivid and clear. From the beginning, Gabe, I've felt like something wasn't right about this. Now, I'm sure of it. If you'd known my dad and his meticulousness about his

163

boats, you would know that this could not have been an accident. Gabe, as crazy as it sounds, I-I think someone may have murdered my family."

Gabe reached for her hand and held it tight. He knew things about dreams and grief and the stages one had to go through to get to acceptance. Lord knows he'd been through it too many times, not just when he lost his parents but also when he'd lost his friends and Seal Team members during the war.

"Sweetie," he said gently, "just try to ride out the feelings. There will be lots of them."

"No," she said, shaking her head." You don't understand. I have to figure this out. I have to know the truth. There's something that's just not right here, Gabe. None of this makes sense. My father was obsessed with safety. He would have never let this happen."

He decided not to reason with her right then. To do so could short circuit her process. It was better to let her explore all the dark corners and ferret out all the questions and the doubts. They sat quietly for a minute, each lost in their thoughts. Finally, he got up, refilled her drink, went to the kitchen, and made two plates. When he returned, she seemed to have her emotions better under control. They shared the simple meal sitting on the floor in front of the coffee table, making small talk about the days since he'd seen her.

When they finished dinner, he noticed the fatigue in her eyes, the satisfaction of a good meal, and the effects of the bourbon taking its toll. When he suggested she go to bed, she didn't protest, and as he tucked her in, he resisted the urge to crawl in beside her. Instead, he put the plates in the sink, locked the doors, and lay down on the couch. When the eastern sky had shown the first light, and he realized she had slept through the night, he slipped out the back door and went up to the farm to take care of the animals.

When Kennedy opened her eyes, the bright morning light was streaming through her bedroom windows. And, though she had missed the sunrise, she was elated the dreams had not tortured her during the night. Maybe now that she had recognized the message, the dreams would cease to haunt her. She felt a new hope that perhaps she had a chance to rid herself of these terrible dreams and the lingering after-effects.

She pondered the new life she had built at the Oasis and what the future might hold. The thought was not intimidating but full of promise. She could do whatever she wanted for the first time in a long time.

As much as she had loved her parents, she had pursued law to please them, especially her father. She harbored no anger at them for pushing her to fulfill their dreams for her. It's just that she hadn't developed her own dreams for herself.

At that moment, she realized that she would never return to practicing law. After the tragedy and before she'd left Miami, she'd asked the firm for an extended leave of absence. They had told her to take all the time she needed, but she knew she would never return to Miami. While practicing law had been rewarding, it was a demanding career. Even though she had made a good living at it, she realized she had dreaded almost every day.

She had been an excellent lawyer like they had told her she would be, but she had never enjoyed it, at least not as her father and brother did. They lived, ate, and breathed the law. She had admired their enthusiasm, dedication, and tenaciousness, but she hadn't loved the law the way they did.

Her mind finally drifted away from the mundane contemplations that had ruled her past. She hadn't realized how isolated the dreams had made her feel until she had shared them with Adsila and Gabe. But now, at least, she didn't feel alone in her grief anymore.

When she'd come to the Oasis, running from the pain and the anguish, she hadn't expected to find a life here. Buying the cabin had been an act of desperation, a way to escape the agony of her profound loss. She'd thought no further than her arrival, that in itself seemingly enough to save her. But she had felt God's hand upon her from the moment she arrived. The place, these people, and their kindness had all come together to rescue her from the despair that had threatened to swallow her whole. Now she could not imagine a life without it all.

She was now faced with an exceedingly difficult decision. To get to the truth about what had happened to her family, she knew she could not do it from there. She would have to leave her sanctuary, the place that had saved her soul, and walk willingly back into the worst pain and suffering she had ever known. The thought of it tore at her insides. How could she possibly do it?

And then there was Gabe. She had never known a man as good and as kind as he was to her. God had brought them together to heal each other, that she was sure of, and now that they'd finally seen their way through to building something together, she would walk away, at least for a while. He wouldn't understand, and he wouldn't want her to go. Would he wait for her? She hoped so, but she wasn't sure. He had his own demons to fight. He couldn't fight hers too.

The thought of leaving them all, even for a while, was almost unbearable, but she knew she would never be whole if she didn't do this. She had no plan, much like when she had come there, and when she closed her suitcase, she was consumed with fear and doubts. After she had tidied the cabin, taken one last look around, and locked the door behind her, she hit the road, knowing she was bound for hell.

Chapter Twelve

"Then you will know the truth and the truth will set you free." John 8:32

G abe pulled up to the back of the cabin but Kennedy's Jeep was nowhere in sight. Assuming she was running an errand in town, he figured she had left the back door open for him, as she usually did. When he turned the knob and realized the door was locked, he got a bad feeling in his gut. He walked around to the river side of the cabin to find the door there was locked too. He peered through the windows on the porch but could see nothing amiss inside. Still, he had a nagging feeling that something about the scene wasn't right, not right at all.

Kennedy checked into her hotel on a busy mid-week afternoon. The semi-circular drive in front of the hotel was alive with expensive sports cars and women in designer outfits. She had forgotten what a fast-paced international city Miami was. It was worlds away from the Oasis.

It had been a long and stressful drive, and she was eager to get settled into her room. She'd been on the phone throughout the drive, trying to set appointments with the state attorney and the investigators involved in the case. Over the past few weeks, she'd received calls from her parent's estate attorney, James Orr, and she had let them go to voicemail. She couldn't bear thinking about her parents or talking about their affairs. She finally checked her messages and found that a close friend of her brothers had been trying to reach her also.

Kennedy's condominium on Brickell sat empty, waiting for her to decide whether to keep or sell it. She'd been too traumatized to decide before she left Miami. She'd made a reservation at a hotel near the courthouse and her parent's estate attorney. Though she loved the Art Deco hotels of South Beach, she didn't want to get caught up in the tourist scene.

The valet at the hotel recognized her immediately from her days of visiting the restaurant in the hotel lobby for business lunches and happy hours. He greeted her warmly, and she could see the sympathy he had for her in his eyes. Everyone seemed to know about the deaths of her family with the media coverage that went on for weeks afterward. Being immediately recognized felt unsettling and reminiscent of the days after the tragedy when she had been followed day and night by the press.

Once in her room, she took in the beauty of Biscayne Bay from the balcony windows on the 23rd floor. It was a bittersweet moment as she remembered the days on the water there with her father and her family. The familiar skyline brought back a flood of memories of her life before. The contrast to her life now at the river was startling. Though many memories were good, she had no desire to return to that life.

She knew she should have called Gabe. She'd intended to call him on the drive down but had been busy trying to reach the people she needed to see while she was there. She wasn't sure what his reaction would be, but she knew he must be worried about her by now. She'd already had three missed calls from him. As kind and caring as he was, it was unfair to make him worry any longer. She hadn't realized how nervous she was about calling him until she saw her hand shaking as she dialed, but she could wait no longer.

"Kennedy," he said, a little breathless when he answered, "are you ok? Is everything all right?"

"Yes," she said, the guilt welling up inside of her at the sound of his voice," everything's ok."

"Where are you?" he asked." I've been trying to reach you all day."

"I'm in Miami," she said, wincing thinking about his reaction, "I left this morning,"

"Miami?" he asked. "Why are you in Miami?"

"I have some things I need to do and to work through here, Gabe. I need to settle my parent's affairs, and I've got to get to the bottom of what happened to them. I'll never be able to move on if I don't."

"I understand, Kennedy, I really do. I'm just not sure running down there, spur of the moment, and not telling anyone where you are going is the best way to go about it," he said, his voice a little stern.

"I know, you're right; I'm sorry," she said. "It's just that when I woke up, I finally realized I needed to do this. I should have told you before I left, but I just decided to come down here this morning, and I was anxious to get on the road."

"I just don't like you being down there alone. It worries me. Where are you staying? Do you want me to come down there?" he asked.

She smiled; he was always trying to look after her. "No, It's ok," she said. "I'm at a hotel on Brickell. I'll text you the address. I'm fine. I'm a big girl, and I grew up here. I know this city like the back of my hand. I'm ok, really. Don't worry about me."

"Well, I don't like it, but I understand. How long will you be down there?" he asked.

169

"I'm not sure," she said," at least a few days, maybe longer. I'm going to meet with the investigators on the case and with the estate attorney. I need to get some things wrapped up with that."

"Ok, well, I think you should trust that the people working on this thing will get to the bottom of it, and I still don't like you being there alone. Call me if you need anything and promise me you'll stay in touch," he said.

"I will," she said. "I promise."

There was an awkward pause before they hung up, neither of them knowing how to end the conversation. When she heard him finally disconnect, her heart constricted a little. She missed him already.

She realized the nagging of the questions in her mind had gotten the best of her. Until she had answers, she wouldn't be able to rest or move on. None of it made sense. Not the fire onboard that raged out of control, destroying the boat and taking the lives of everyone. And not the failure of all the safety equipment she was sure her dad had installed on the boat. Someone had to have started the fire intending to kill them all. She had so many questions but no answers. But she knew in her heart it must have been foul play.

Her father would have checked everything on the boat the day before they planned to go to sea. They were heading to Bimini in the Bahamas, and while it was only a 50-mile trip, he would have prepared carefully as he always did. The trip typically only took about two hours, and they had made it many times through the years. He had been excited to make the journey on his new yacht with the entire family onboard. As always, safety precautions would have been of paramount importance to him.

As she thought through all these unanswered questions, her mind wandered to what was on her schedule the next day. She had set a ten o'clock meeting with the detective in charge of her family's case and the state attorney, who had been a close friend to her father. She wanted someone in the room whom she felt she could trust and who would look out for her best interests. She hoped they could give her an update on their investigation and some insights into what may have happened. She didn't know what to expect from the meeting. She was hoping to get something, anything to go on.

She hadn't heard from the estate attorney yet but was sure she would see him in the next couple of days. She wasn't looking forward to that meeting. Hearing about the final disposition of her parent's estate would be a difficult time for her in the grieving process, and she wasn't sure she was ready to face it. If she could get away with delaying for a while, she might. She already had a lot on her plate.

She was, however, looking forward to seeing her brother's best friend, Hayden. Though she had never been particularly fond of him and his country club style, at least he was a connection to her brother, and the voicemail messages he had left for her had been genuinely kind and sympathetic. Spending time with someone who knew her family and shared her grief would be comforting. They were to meet at the upscale steak house across from her hotel for lunch, where she had spent many good times with her family. She was sure being there would bring back a flood of memories. Since she'd left Miami so soon after she lost her family, she hadn't had many experiences where people and places reminded her of them. She hoped she could hold it together.

The morning came quickly as she, apparently exhausted, had slept later than she intended to. She had slept through the night again and had not experienced the nightmares that had plagued her for months. It was a welcome relief as she needed her energy and a sharp mind to get through the meetings she had planned. With time running short, she made a quick cup of coffee in the room, forgoing her craving for a cafe con leche from her favorite coffee shop around the corner.

She'd mainly brought business clothes with her and, having packed hastily, hadn't thought about what she would wear to her meetings. Now, faced with the decision, she chose her navy blue pinstripe suit. To her, it had always been the power suit she chose for important meetings where she wanted to make a bold impression. Today was no exception. She wanted them to know that in getting to the bottom of what happened to her parents, she meant business. She put on a discrete set of diamond jewelry, a gift from her parents when she graduated law school, made quick work of her make-up, swept her hair up into her signature ponytail, and dashed down to the lobby to catch her Uber.

The state attorney's office downtown was new and modern and was juxtaposed with the new and equally contemporary Courthouse. The two buildings looked more like art museums than they did utilitarian towers of justice, she thought, as she rode the elevator to the top floor.

"Good morning," she said as she approached the receptionist. "I'm Kennedy Klark. I have a ten o'clock meeting with Patrick Price."

"Good morning," the pleasant young woman said. "I'll let him know you're here."

Kennedy paced around the reception area and then went to stand by the window overlooking downtown Miami while she checked her notes and looked through the questions she had written on a legal pad. She noticed her palms were sweaty, and she was nervous. It wasn't like her.

"Ms. Klark, I can take you back now," the young girl said with a smile. Kennedy followed the receptionist to a large conference room where the state attorney and lead detective were already seated at the table. Both men rose when she came into the room.

"Good morning, Kennedy, I'm Patrick Price," he said as he extended his hand. "I'm so very sorry for your loss. I knew your father well. We had a mutual respect that grew into a good friendship through the years. I'm also sorry we are meeting under these circumstances." He paused and turned towards the other man. "This is the lead detective on your family's case, Alejandro Martinez."

"Just call me Alex, Ms. Klark," the detective said as he smiled at her.

"Thank you," she said. "Please just call me Kennedy." Everyone was quiet for a moment, the situation rather tense and awkward.

"Well, let's all sit down, shall we?" Patrick said, pulling out Kennedy's chair. "I think it might be beneficial to start with Detective Martinez giving us the details of what his investigation has revealed so far."

"Let me just say first, Kennedy, that I too am sorry for your loss. You have my deepest sympathy. I didn't know your father personally, but I have only heard good things about him as an attorney and a family man," the detective said.

"Thank you," Kennedy said as she looked into his kind eyes. She could tell his sympathy was genuine. "I appreciate you both taking the time to meet with me today."

The detective opened up his accordion file and took out individual legal files labeled and color-coded. Kennedy assumed they contained notes, reports, and sworn statements. And perhaps photographs of the scene and drawings. She hadn't practiced criminal law, but she had grown up with a father who did. While she watched the detective preparing to speak, she remembered sitting with her dad in his office many years before watching him organize his files. She shut her eyes for a brief second to blot out the memory. She didn't want to lose her composure.

"Kennedy, it's difficult to know where to begin. Patrick has told me that you are here seeking answers. That is why I feel I should start with the fact that we don't have any. The fire almost completely destroyed your father's yacht. The remnants of what was left have not revealed much to assist us in how this happened. The arson investigation team's formal report has determined the fire to be an accident. We have a team of detectives who have worked under my direction on this case and have come to the same conclusion. We provided these reports to the insurance company via their request by subpoena. My understanding is that their separate investigation has not revealed anything more." The detective lowered his eyes and said," I am sorry, we don't have any more to add."

"If I may interject," Patrick said. "Kennedy, because of my relationship with your father, I've reviewed all of the reports. I've inquired as to the depth of the investigation, and it appears the Coral Gables Police Department has dotted all their i's and crossed all their t's. The scope of the damage to the yacht provided a complex landscape for the investigation, and the addition of water was an added hindrance to finding out the source of the fire."

"If I may, I do have some questions," Kennedy said.

"Of course," the detective said. "I'll answer anything I can for you."

"My father was very meticulous about everything he did, especially regarding the care of his boats. This particular yacht was my father's dream boat. He told my brother and me that he was purchasing it because of the excellent safety systems. He knew a fire

174

was a serious threat on a boat. He always checked everything before he took his boats out, especially for a trip like this one to the Bahamas. Were those involved in the investigation able to determine where the fire started? Wouldn't the fire alarms on the boat have alerted my family to the issue? Why were they unable to get off the boat? It all doesn't make sense to me," Kennedy said, her voice weakening with a slight tremble.

"All those questions are good, and I have asked them myself. It comes down to the fact that the fire almost completely destroyed the yacht, and there was very little evidence to lead to the discovery of how the fire started." Alex paused for a moment, letting that sink in."Kennedy, I'm thinking this is either an accident or the perfect crime; that said, without much more, we won't be able to determine which it is."

"I know this will sound irrational, but I believe someone murdered my parents and brother," Kennedy confessed. "The problem is I have no proof. I just have a gut feeling that something isn't right here."

Alex leaned in and spoke quietly, "Unfortunately, that isn't enough to go on. I know you know that, Kennedy. We have looked at every angle. Nothing seems out of place or indicative of any trouble leading to a crime."

"I understand, Alex. I get it," she said, her voice just above a whisper.

"Your dad was an amazing man," Patrick said, "and your mom a lovely woman. I didn't know your brother, but I knew he was following in your father's footsteps in the law firm. I'd been looking forward to seeing his development as a trial attorney. Kennedy, I know this is hard. If it was an accident, it is a terrible disaster. If it was something more sinister, then even more so of a tragedy. I know closure is so needed and important in situations such as this.

We had hoped to provide that for you, but we can't. We can only pray that answers will present themselves through circumstances we aren't aware of at this time. I can confirm that everything we could do to find out what happened we did, and the investigation has come up cold."

Kennedy closed her eyes and sighed. She realized she had come here prepared to fight, but there was nothing to fight about. These men were the professionals Gabe had told her they would be. They wanted to help her and wished they had answers for her. Not having any made her feel empty and devastated.

Kennedy gathered herself together and stood. "Thank you both for your time this morning and for meeting with me. I appreciate all you have done to discover what happened on that yacht and what happened to my family. Even though there are no real answers, I feel comforted by your true efforts and professional dedication."

They all shook hands, and the two men escorted her to the door. The discouragement she felt was nearly overwhelming. How would she ever be able to move on from this with no answers? She just didn't know.

———

Hayden Dunworthy was already seated at his regular table and was ordering his second martini when she arrived at the restaurant. As she approached him, he immediately stood and greeted her with a warm hug and a kiss on each cheek. Well-acquainted with social graces, he pulled out her chair, took her bag for her, and waited until she was seated to sit back down.

"It is good to see you, Koko; you look well," he said. "I always just thought of you as Liam's little sister. I guess I hadn't realized you were all grown up," he said, giving her the once over.

She ignored his comment. It was quintessential Hayden. "I want to apologize right up front," Kennedy said. "I should have returned your calls sooner, and I also want to thank you for caring about me and checking in on me. I'm doing ok."

"Please don't apologize. I know this must be a very difficult time, and I just wanted to make sure you knew I was thinking about you. I heard you left town pretty quick after the tragedy. Are you getting settled somewhere? How long will you be in Miami?" he asked.

"Honestly, Hayden, I've had some very tough moments. It's all still so surreal. I think I was in shock for a while, and the feelings are starting to emerge slowly. I've felt very alone at times and afraid. But I found a place in North Florida that I like, and it helps to be in a different place without the memories I have here. It helps that the landscape is different, the people are new, and no one knows my family. I'm getting settled, and as each day goes by, I'm adjusting to the loss. I'm here for just a few days. I'm here to look into what happened to my brother and my parents and to get some things settled," she said.

They stopped talking for a few minutes as the server took their order. "Do you want a glass of wine with your salad?" Hayden asked. "They have a new sauvignon blanc by the glass that is really good."

"That would be lovely," she said as she smiled at the server. "I just left a meeting with the lead detective and the state attorney. They don't know what happened to my family. The fire destroyed the yacht, so there isn't much to go on. The authorities have decided that the whole incident and their deaths were an accident," she said.

"The news media here is still obsessed with the case and have been reporting that there is no real way to determine what happened that night," he said as he took a long drink of his martini. "I don't mean to be callous, but everyone is saying you will inherit a fortune. Do you know how much yet?"

At first, she thought to ignore what others might have considered a rude comment since she knew Hayden didn't have much of a filter. It was one reason why she hadn't been too fond of him through the years. But since he had been kind enough to check up on her these last weeks, she decided to cut him a break.

"Hayden, you've been my brother's best friend since kindergarten. It's ok to say what is on your mind; I know you aren't one to mince words. I guess you're probably right, though I don't know for sure. My father never discussed finances with me," Kennedy said.

"Well, he did with your brother Liam. I'm surprised he didn't discuss these matters with you. Maybe, he decided to when Liam was spending all that money last year," Hayden said. "I kept telling him to slow down; he was racing in the fast lane and spending money like a drunken sailor. Your dad was very conservative and wasn't happy at all. Your father worked hard, and he was cautious with his money."

Kennedy was stunned. "What? I wasn't aware of any of this. What was going on?"

"Oh, I thought you knew. I guess the martinis have made me a little loose-lipped." Hayden put down his drink and realized he better not order a third as he was getting sloppy. "Your brother had become cozy with some guys who were living large, and your father disapproved. He wanted to know where Hayden was getting the money to run with these guys. He was making good money in the law firm, but not that kind of money."

"Hayden do you think this could this have something to do with what happened on the yacht?" Kennedy asked.

"Oh, I don't know. I hadn't thought of that. Liam didn't like your father telling him what to do, and they had a few heated conversations about it. Liam mentioned it to me on several occasions over a few beers at the club." He drained the rest of his martini. "I tried to talk some sense into him too. Look, I like to have a good time, and I've been known to knock back one too many drinks on occasion or, well, on most occasions. But these dudes were into a lot more than that. I didn't want Liam around them either."

Kennedy's head was spinning. Though she had never been close to her brother, she knew he had a reputation as a carouser and liked the company of beautiful women. She hadn't known that his lifestyle had gotten out of hand, and her father was distressed about it.

Kennedy felt like she may be onto something now, so she pressed a little. "Hayden, thanks for being so forthright about all this. Is there anything else that stands out to you? Anything else about my brother in the past year?" she asked.

"You know, I have been wondering about a few things since he died. One time, in particular, he was on the phone at the pub out at the club. The club has a rule that you can't use your phone during lunch and dinner hours, even in casual areas. He was in a heated conversation with someone, and one of the employees had to ask him to get off the phone or leave. He ended the call but laid into the poor club guy with a vengeance. It was not like your brother; Liam was pretty easygoing. It was weird behavior," Hayden said. "I asked him who he had been talking to, but he didn't answer. I asked him why he had gotten so out of hand with the employee, and I thought he would take it all out on me next by the look on his face. We had never had a fight in our entire friendship of 35 years. It was odd that he reacted that way."

Kennedy could not imagine what she was hearing about her brother. This seemed so out of character for him. "If anything else comes to your mind, Hayden, would you please let me know?" Kennedy asked.

"Yes, of course, I will. Koko, I just want to tell you again how sorry I am that all of this happened. I hope you can find some peace and healing in North Florida. Just remember there are people here who care about you. I understand it is difficult to be here and painful, but if and when you visit again, please let me know. I would love to see you. And please know that I am here if you need me. I know you think of me as a spoiled rich kid, but I do have a heart. I loved your brother, and I will always be here for you," Hayden said with his voice shaking.

"I know, Hayden," Kennedy said with tears in her eyes. "Thank you for being there for me. It means more than you know."

When Kennedy looked at her phone the following day, she realized she had missed a call from the estate attorney. She again had stayed in bed longer than she wanted to and had slept well with no dreams waking her and terrorizing her in the wee hours of the morning.

The voicemail left by the estate attorney asked if she could be available for a 3 pm meeting that afternoon. With it barely being 9 am, Kennedy was glad to have a little downtime before the meeting and a chance to think through questions she might want to ask. She decided to order some breakfast and call Gabe to touch base.

"Hey," she said when she heard his voice, not realizing how much she missed him until she heard his deep Southern accent.

"Hey," he said. "I was just wondering about you. How's it going there?"

"It's going ok but I'm not finding out much, unfortunately. They have no idea what happened on the boat. All arrows point to an accident, but I'm still not convinced. Found out some weird stuff about my brother that I'll fill you in on later," she said. "Tell me what's going on in your world?"

"Well, I can't say there's too much to report. Not much changes around here from day to day," he said with a chuckle. "Everyone is worried about you, though, and wants you to come home." She smiled, the word "home" sitting nicely on her soul. She missed her life there and the little cabin in the Oasis. "Do you think you will be doing that soon?" he asked.

"Well, I have a few more things I need to do down here before I head back. I have a meeting with the estate attorney this afternoon. It will be a big relief to get that one behind me," she said.

"I understand that," he said, and she realized he had been through the same thing after his parents had passed. "I'm sure your dad had everything set up well. Hopefully, you'll be able to get things settled without much trouble. I'm headed out tomorrow afternoon to my buddy's hunt camp. We get together out there a few times a year and drink whiskey and tell lies," he said with a laugh, and she laughed with him. "I'll be back on Sunday. But I'll have my cell phone if you need anything." There was a long pause, and he said, finally, "I miss you, Kennedy, very much. I want you to come home soon."

She felt the tears spring to her eyes, and her voice caught in her throat." I miss you too, Gabe," she whispered." I'll see you soon, I promise."

She had never met James Orr, her parents' estate attorney, but he seemed to be a kind and compassionate man. He had expressed his condolences to her eloquently though she guessed he'd had a lot of practice in doing that. Still, she liked his calm and reassuring demeanor; he seemed very thorough and to the point.

"Kennedy," he said, "as the sole heir to your parent's estate and your brother's, you will receive all of the assets, properties, and all proceeds from the three life insurance policies, though that may take a while until the investigation into the, ah, accident is complete."

"Three policies?" she asked. "Why three?"

"Your parents each had one, and your brother had one as well. Your father was a practical man, and your brother was a valuable asset to the law firm. It made sense to insure him."

"Oh," she said. "I hadn't realized that."

"There is also the matter of the insurance proceeds on the boat, but that will be a while, I imagine. Anyway, everything in the estate trusts otherwise will be conveyed to you immediately. Here is a summary of all of the assets. This does not include the personal belongings of your parents and brother such as furniture, jewelry, etc.," he said as he slid the paperwork over to Kennedy. To say she was surprised at the numbers was an understatement. She'd had no idea her parents had possessed that much wealth.

"There is one exception in the will. There is a trust set aside by your father if the named beneficiary of the trust is ever in need of it."

Kennedy looked up, surprised. "May I know who the beneficiary is?" she asked.

"Yes," he said as he looked over his glasses. "I know this may come as a surprise to you, Kennedy, but you have a living grandmother."

Chapter Thirteen

"For where two or three gather in my name, there am I with them." Matthew 18:20

Kat Maguire sipped her morning coffee on the balcony of her high-rise condo on Key Biscayne overlooking the blue-green waters of the Atlantic Ocean. From her vantage point in the penthouse, she could see, on a clear day, from Cape Florida Lighthouse almost to Fisher Island. Today was such a day, the South Florida sun bright and the view unobscured by any haze.

If there was any one word to describe her, it could have been something as simple as magnanimous or as complex as labyrinthine. She was those things and everything in between. Kat Maguire had needed no one or anything to define her, though. She'd been around too many blocks for that.

At nearly 79, she barely looked a day over 60. Though she'd lived a life of luxury and ease, her good looks were more a product of her superior genes than her lifestyle. She'd never seen a day on a diet or been under a plastic surgeon's knife, but she could still turn the heads of younger men and raise the ire of envious women.

It wasn't just her good looks, though, that made her so distinctive. Even with her height, her perfect posture, and her classic beauty, her presence commanded the most attention. She could have graced the cover of any fashion magazine; editors had asked many times, but mundane flattery held no appeal to her. She had wanted to live a life of more importance.

The sound of the doorman buzzing her snapped her out of her ethereal state. She felt annoyed. There was no reason to interrupt her morning with the arrival of a package or such thing. Whatever he was bothering her about could have waited until after lunch.

"Yes," she snapped into the intercom," what is it?"

"I'm sorry to bother you, Ms. Maguire, but you have someone here to see you," the doorman blurted out.

"Oh," she said, looking at her watch. "At this hour? Who is it?"

"She says she's a relative. Would you like to see her on camera?" he said as he turned the camera around.

Kat recognized her immediately. "Please send her up."

Kennedy stood in front of her grandmother's door, not knowing who or what to expect. She did not know this woman or at least did not remember her if she had as a child. When she had first learned she had a close, living relative, she was elated at the idea. Now, as she stood there, she was suddenly terrified. So many questions filled her mind to which she needed answers.

She knocked lightly on the door, and as a minute passed, she wondered if anyone had heard her. As she raised her hand to knock again, the door suddenly opened, and Kennedy laid eyes on a woman who was seemingly an older version of herself. The resemblance was startling.

Though Kennedy had received her black Irish coloring from her father, she had clearly inherited everything else about her physical makeup from her grandmother. At an almost identical height, the two women looked each other eye to eye, the mirrored image of each other reflecting the high cheekbones and facial structure that one can only achieve through perfect genetics. Everything from their graceful shoulders to their slim hips was

185

twin-like. It would have been obvious to anyone seeing them together that they were closely related.

"Kennedy," Kat said softly as she held out her hand. "I was hoping you would come."

_____

The two women sat quietly across from one another for a few minutes. Kat spoke first.

"How are you holding up, darling?" she asked." How are you enduring all of this?"

"I'm doing ok," Kennedy said. "I'm getting through it."

"Well, of course, you are," Kat said as she got up and went to the kitchen. Moments later, she was back with two glasses of champagne. "You must have a lot of questions," she said as she handed one to Kennedy.

"I do, but I have no idea where to begin," Kennedy said as she took a sip of her champagne. _Cristal_, she thought, she'd know it anywhere.

"Well, I can give you the short version if you'd like," Kat said as she eyed Kennedy over the rim of her glass. "I was a terrible mother, and your mother hated me for it. Being banished from your life and your brother's life was how she chose to punish me."

Kennedy thought about that for a moment. "Well, I loved my mother," she said with a sigh, "and I probably shouldn't be saying this, especially now, but as long as we are being honest, I can't say she was a perfect one either."

"I'm afraid the apple never falls far from the tree, my darling," Kat said as she shrugged. "I think she wanted to be better; she just had a horrible role model." The two women were quiet for a minute, sipping champagne and thinking about things.

"How is it that I never knew you were still alive, and all the while, you were right here in Key Biscayne?" Kennedy asked.

"By design," Kat said. "When your mother and I became estranged, your grandfather, Liam O'Brien, had recently passed away, and I had just moved here from Connecticut. I began using my maiden name, Maguire, to save the family from scrutiny. No one was the wiser." She paused, then went on." I think she did the best she could, Kennedy. She was certainly attentive to Liam when he was a baby. You know, I was allowed to see him until you were born. That's when everything changed. I think when she had you, the realities of her relationship with me and her childhood became overwhelming. She didn't know how to have a relationship with you, and I don't think she trusted me not to abandon you like she felt I abandoned her."

"Did you?" Kennedy asked. "Abandon her?"

"I certainly wasn't around much when she was a child. I'll admit that. I was selfish and self-centered and wanted to see the world without having a child in tow. I let the nuns and the nannies raise her. I didn't realize how wretched things were for her at the time. My childhood wasn't much different, though. I should have known," Kat said as she sipped her champagne. "She did contact me, you know, right before the accident."

"Really?" Kennedy asked. "What did she want?"

"I don't know," Kat said. "She just said she wanted to see me. Of course, I agreed, but it never happened. She died before we were able to meet."

"That's sad," Kennedy said." Maybe you two could have reconciled."

Kat smiled and nodded. "I was hoping for that." They were both quiet again, thinking things through. "So tell me about your life, my darling; where are you living now? I've kept tabs on you for a long time, but I know you left town after the accident."

"I had to go," she said." It was just so terrible after the tragedy. I had no one to help me, and it was all so overwhelming. The press followed me and hounded me day and night. They went to the law firm where I worked and somehow got through the doorman at my condo. I found a little cabin for sale in the woods in North Florida and bought it sight unseen. I just took off," she said, as her voice cracked." But I like it there. The people up there are very nice, and the place is beautiful. And it doesn't remind me of here and my family."

Kat had gotten up and gone to sit next to her granddaughter. She put her arms around her and pulled her close. "I'm sorry; I should have reached out to you right away. I wanted to; I just didn't want to add to your confusion. I thought when things settled down; maybe we could get to know one another. Then you were gone. I'd been hoping you would come once you found out about me."

Kennedy melted into her grandmother's arms, and the feeling of belonging there nearly overwhelmed her. She was suddenly profoundly sad for all the lost years and wasted time. Something shifted in her soul as her grandmother held her as she cried. She suddenly felt she belonged to someone again, and a little piece of her broken heart mended itself. They sat like that for a long time, Kat rocking her granddaughter for the first time in her 35 years, both women trying to get back a little of the time they had lost.

A little while later, Kat placed her hands on her granddaughter's shoulders and looked her in the eyes. "Is there anything you need, my darling, anything at all? Money? A place to stay while you're here in Miami?"

"No, I'm ok, really I am," Kennedy said. "I just have a few more things to get done here in town, and then I'm going back to North Florida."

Kat was quiet for a moment. "What is your schedule like for the rest of the day?" she asked. "Can you stay awhile? I can order up some lunch, and we can spend some time together."

"I'd like that," Kennedy said as she smiled." There's just one thing, though."

"What's that?" Kat asked as she stopped and cocked her head.

"What shall I call you?"

Kat laughed and gave her a wink. "Anything but Grandma."

After Kennedy left in the afternoon, Kat thought back on the time she had spent with her that day and was overwhelmed by the maternal instinct she had felt upon meeting her granddaughter. How could it be, she wondered, that she had never felt that for her own daughter? She wouldn't try to fool anyone into believing she hadn't been a wretched example of a mother. It would have been easy to do and place the blame on her daughter, especially now that she was gone. But if Kat was anything, she was a blunt realist. Realizing now that her granddaughter possessed that same attribute, though softer around the edges, made the idea of trying to pretend things had been any different a futile one.

When she'd first laid eyes on Kennedy, she'd seen a vision of herself, not just in their physical similarities but in how she carried herself. Kennedy possessed a strong internal spirit and an iron backbone but what Kat was most inspired by was Kennedy's obvious good heart and compassion. It had taken old age for Kat to find that in herself.

189

She was sure she had Keegan to thank for that. He clearly had been a wonderful father to her and had headed off the selfish indifference that had haunted the family bloodline of mothers for over three generations. Kat had never had much of a relationship with her father; he had left the raising, or lack thereof, sadly to her mother. But she had never blamed her mother for their detached relationship. She was sure her grandmother had been quite the same. She was relieved to see that Keegan had broken what seemed to be a generational curse.

As she and Kennedy spent the day together, sharing a meal and syncing up their lives, it was as though they had gotten back at least some of the 35 years they had lost. When Kennedy relaxed with her, Kat marveled at her granddaughter's wit and intelligence. She knew that Keegan had wanted Kennedy to join his law firm when she graduated from law school, but she had been proud to discover that Kennedy had forged her own successful path. That would have been enough to tell Kat everything she needed to know about her granddaughter.

Through the years, Keegan had, secretly, stayed in touch with her, and she was sure Keegan had finally persuaded Mary Theresa to reconcile with her mother. Though he knew she had wealth, he had always made it clear that Kat could come to him if she ever needed anything. He often expressed his sadness she did not know her grandchildren but betraying Mary Theresa's wishes to keep them from their grandmother was a line he had not been willing to cross. She was sure he had wanted Kat to get to know her grandchildren while she still had some time on this earth.

When Kennedy told her about the trust her father had left for her, it lifted her heart. She didn't need it, but it was one of the kindest gestures anyone had ever made toward her. After much discussion, she and Kennedy had decided to donate the money to the University of Miami Law School in her father's name. Though he was not an alumnus, he was a local legend in the field of law, and memorializing him there seemed like the right thing to do.

When Kat said goodbye to her granddaughter that afternoon, it had been one of her life's happiest and saddest moments. Though she was sure they had developed a close bond in the short time they had known each other, she was realistic enough to know that with Kennedy heading back to North Florida soon, their time together would be limited.

Kennedy had told her all about the cabin and her life up on the river. She was relieved that Kennedy was happy there and had met people who seemed good friends to her. She was most optimistic, though, to hear that Kennedy had a man in her life. Though she had downplayed the relationship, she could tell it was more than she was letting on and that he cared enough to look after her. She'd also told her about the cabin's origin and the O'Brien names on the documents, and though Kennedy did not have the documents with her, one name had seemed to match her late husband's. She was unaware of any land sale in North Florida he would have been a part of, but she promised to contact her husband's only living sibling, a sister, to see if she knew anything. Kat was happy they had that as a thread they could hang onto to build on their new and fledgling relationship. Above all, she knew that now that she had Kennedy in her life, she didn't want to let her go.

───────────

As Kennedy crossed Biscayne Bay, over the Rickenbacker causeway, she felt a range of emotions, not the least of which was relief. Knowing she was not alone in this world seemed to ground her again and had closed an echoing hole in her heart. The time she'd spent with her grandmother that afternoon had answered so many questions for her. She felt that she was on the path to becoming a whole person and realized that before today, she'd never known that she wasn't one.

191

As she looked out over the blue-green waters of Biscayne Bay, she realized, and was amazed at the thought, that all the while she was growing up and especially as an adult living and working downtown, her grandmother had been just across the bay. In trying to understand her mother's thinking, she wondered why, after all these years, she had contacted her grandmother shortly before she died. Had she wanted to reconcile? Kennedy was sure she would never know. She was a bit angry at the years her mother had stolen from her and her grandmother and that, if her parents had not died, she might have never known her. It was an odd twist of events.

Her original plan was to go to her parent's home on her way out of town in the morning. But after visiting her grandmother, she decided to go straight there. That way, she could leave for the river in the morning after the crush of rush hour and be home well before dark. She was getting eager to get home and back in her safe haven at the cabin. She was oddly curious to face being in the house again alone, without her family. It would not be easy, but she thought facing some stark realities might be a big step toward healing. The pragmatic part of her knew that eventually, she would need to sell the home she'd grown up in. As hard as it was to think about, she knew the house would soon become an albatross for her, and with the knowledge she would never come back to Miami to live, it served no purpose in her life now.

It was late afternoon, and the traffic getting over to the Gables was heavy and snarled. What would have normally been about a thirty-minute drive would now take her the better part of an hour, and when she glanced at her watch, she realized she would not arrive there until after six in the evening. Feeling hungry, she stopped for dinner at her favorite Vietnamese restaurant downtown in the Gables. It had been a while since she had any ethnic food as the life at the river did not afford quick take-out or international cuisine. The hostess seated her at her favorite table by the window.

When the owner recognized her, she gave her a warm hug. Though she'd only been gone a few months, sometimes it felt like a lifetime.

The man at the guard house at the entrance of her parent's neighborhood did not recognize the Jeep, but when she rolled down her window, she saw him smile and nod in recognition. She briefly paused as he lifted the gate and let her through. She wound through the beautiful neighborhood of huge homes and finally pulled into the apron of her parent's driveway. She punched the code in on the entry keypad, and the large iron gates swung open to let her in. As her father had taught her, she pulled in just enough for the gates to close but not far enough for anyone to come in behind her. He had always been thinking about safety.

She pulled the Jeep into the garage, shut the door behind her, and entered her parent's home through the side door that led to the kitchen. Once she had disabled the alarm system, she walked through the house, turning on the lights as she went. Everything looked frozen in time as every detail looked the same. Before she left South Florida, she'd arranged for the housekeeper and the gardener, who her parents had employed for years, to remain employed to care for the home and the grounds. From the looks of things, that had been a good decision. There were no newspapers in the driveway or overgrown shrubs to broadcast no one was living there. Inside, the house was clean and fresh and didn't have the feeling it had been closed for months.

She climbed the stairs and went straight to her parent's bedroom and to the location of the hidden safe behind a large hanging mirror in her parent's dressing room. Using a particular method shown to her by her father, she unlatched the mirrored door at the side and swung it open. Finding no signs that the safe had been disturbed, she closed it again, not opening the safe itself. She was not prepared to deal with its contents at that moment. She would have to save that for another visit.

As she walked back into her parent's bedroom, her eyes landed on her mother's writing desk, the memories of her mother sitting there filling her mind. On instinct, she opened drawers, looking through the contents, and in the top right-hand drawer, she found a beautiful, hand-tooled leather-bound journal. Kennedy sat down on her parent's bed and flipped through the pages. Thinking back on her childhood memories, she was sure this is what her mother was doing the many times Kennedy had seen her writing at the desk. The date at the beginning meant there were probably many more, though Kennedy had not seen them in the desk. The thought she could get a glimpse into her mother's most intimate thoughts, and chronicles of her life almost seemed wrong, but she knew there would be answers to many questions for her there. As she flipped through the pages, admiring her mother's perfect and beautiful handwriting, she instinctively went to the last few pages, yearning to see her mother's thoughts during the days leading up to her death. Sentences floated off the page here and there, but one particular paragraph caught her eye:

...At this point, I realize that I must make peace with my own mother. How can I ever expect Kennedy to forgive me for the childhood I gave her if I can't forgive my own mother for the one she gave me? Kennedy was a loving and imaginative child and deserved better than what I gave her. I fear had it not been for Keegan, she would have grown into the cold, empty young woman I was years ago...

Kennedy closed the journal and sat it on the bed beside her. She had read enough of it for now. And as much as she wanted to crawl into her parent's bed and cry, she decided doing so would only rub salt into her wounds. She'd come to the house to look for anything to help her discover what happened to her family, and she had little time. With that thought in mind, she went downstairs, taking the journal with her, to her father's office and began her search there.

Keegan Klark liked organization and things in their place, so it was easy for Kennedy to look through the office for clues. She started with the top drawer of his desk, but there was nothing much there but office supplies. The bottom drawer on the right was just mundane, everyday bills and contracts concerning the house. However, the drawer on the bottom left was locked, and she looked around and through the desk but could not find a key. Perhaps he'd had the key on his key ring, and it had perished with him in the fire, but she knew he would have had a second key hidden somewhere. She needed to find it.

Sitting and thinking about it, she remembered her dad showing her the secret drawer. He'd always told her that if he needed to hide anything important, he would put it there. As a child, she'd been fascinated by it, but she had not thought about it in a long time. She slid off his desk chair onto the floor and crawled up under the desk, looking around and trying to remember precisely the drawer's location. As she pushed and prodded along, she suddenly felt something give, and the drawer released ever so gently, only a tiny portion of its profile protruding from the panel of the desk. She slid the drawer out and crawled back up in the chair where she could set it on the desk. The drawer had a thin, wood top meant to protect its contents, and when she removed it, she was surprised to see an envelope with her name written in her father's handwriting.

She picked up the envelope and carefully opened it not understanding what it might contain. As she unfolded the paper she saw it was a handwritten letter and from the date at the top, she could see it had been written not long before his death:

My Dearest Kennedy,

If you are reading this, something terrible has happened. Not knowing what that would be, I cannot guess your state of mind. What I know is that your brother is in trouble, and I fear for him and all of us.

Your brother has gotten himself involved with some bad actors. I have been assembling evidence of his dealings with these people and some documents I think are related. You will find these in an encrypted file on my desktop computer. The encryption keys are below. Since this does not seem to involve you in any way, I hope you are safe from any harm, but I don't know that for sure. Please be careful. Liam has been acting erratically, and I don't know how deep in he is. I can only tell you that large amounts of money are involved. Whatever he has gotten himself into, it is significant.

I hope that you never read this letter, but if you are, I assume you are as shocked and saddened as I am. Maybe I am dead, and if you are grieving, my heart is with you. I am depending on you to figure this out if I can't. You have always had the most brilliant mind among us, so I know I can count on you.

My Love Always,

Dad

Although the letter was sad and devastating, she knew now what she had suspected for a while. Whatever Liam had gotten himself into had led to her parents' deaths and to his own demise. Feeling determined to finally get to the bottom of things and know the truth, she went right to work. She logged on to her father's computer and found the encrypted files. When she was in, she put a flash drive in the port and started the download. As soon as she was sure the download was progressing with no errors, she left her father's office and went to the key closet in the pantry off the kitchen. It took a few minutes, but after going through all the sets of keys, she finally found them and headed for the back door.

Liam had been living in the carriage house for the last few months as he awaited the completion of his new condo downtown. The developer was way behind on the construction, and Liam had found himself without a place to live after he'd sold his other place. Rather than signing a lease, It had been an easy solution to move into the furnished carriage house. All he'd needed to do was bring his personal items, and everything else had gone into storage. It was only supposed to be for a few weeks, but with construction delays ongoing, it had turned into months.

The carriage house was tidy, so she guessed the housekeeper had been looking after it also. She didn't know what she was looking for, but she figured she would start with his desk drawers to see what might be there. Finding only some pens and a few magazines, she moved on to search his bedroom. His nightstands were fruitless, though interesting, as she noticed he had condoms and marijuana and what looked like the remnants of some cocaine paraphernalia. She wondered how many women Liam had brought to the carriage house while staying there. It would have been easy to do without his parents noticing since it had its own entrance through a back gate and was far enough from the house he would not have had to worry about them hearing anything.

She rifled through his bathroom medicine cabinet, finding a host of prescription drugs but nothing else of interest. The kitchen was sparse as she was sure he did little there besides make coffee. She started to go when something silver on the couch caught her eye. When she pulled back the cushion, she saw Liam's laptop wedged down into the side of the sofa, only the top of it visible. She wrestled it out and tucked it under her arm. With the place being small, there weren't very many places to look for things, so having exhausted her search, she decided to go, locking the door behind her as she left.

When she got back to her father's office, she checked the flash drives and saw the files were there. She pulled them from their ports and dropped them in her large tote along with Liam's laptop. As she was finishing and gathering her things, she remembered the locked drawer and tried the keys she had found in the hidden drawer. On the third try, the lock turned, and the drawer opened. Inside were files that contained mostly titles to cars, boats, and other important documentation, but what caught her eye was the dark metal object back behind the last file. Kennedy reached in and pulled out her father's H&K .40 caliber handgun, and after turning it over in her hand, she dropped it into her bag.

Chapter Fourteen

"He will call on me, and I will answer him; I will be with him in trouble, I will deliver him and honor him." Psalm 91:15

G abe loaded up his hunting gear and military duffle into the back seat of his truck, locked up the farmhouse, and went up to the barn to double-check the feed supplies. Although he'd stocked everything up a couple of days ago, he wanted to ensure there was plenty there to get through the next few days. One of the local boys working for Gabe part-time after school would feed and water the animals and look after the farm while he was gone. Even though it was only for a few days, he wanted to make sure there were no hiccups, and he'd asked Finn to look in on things here and there to be sure. When he was satisfied everything was in order he checked the tie downs on the trailer carrying his ATV and got in his truck and headed out, bound for the hunt camp.

It was getting late in the afternoon, and Gabe was running a little behind. Since the storm, the sawmill orders had kept him busy from morning to night. But today, he was knocking off early so he could get up to the hunt camp well before dark. He didn't want to miss the festivities the men shared the first night of camp, and he needed a break from the relentless work. Without Kennedy, he had no distractions and no work to do at the cabin.

He pulled through the farm's front entrance, got out, and pulled the gate shut behind him. He'd given the boy the keys to the farm truck and parked it inside the locked entrance. That way, he could hop the gate and drive up to the barn when he came to feed the animals, and Gabe would have peace of mind that the farm was secure. Once the gate was locked, he turned down the lane and headed to Finn's cabin. As he approached, he saw Finn was on his tractor bush hogging the easement in front of his property. He pulled to a halt when he saw Gabe coming down the road.

"Headed out!" Gabe yelled over the noise as he pulled up alongside the tractor. "You've got your key to the gate?"

Finn gave him a thumbs up and a wave of his hat, and Gabe started forward again, navigating the truck around the bend to the right and headed down the lime rock lane, under the oak canopy, toward the main road. When he passed the entrance into Kennedy's property and cabin, his heart constricted a little. He missed her.

If he were honest with himself, he was worried. Not just for her safety, which he knew was probably just his protective instincts kicking in, but he was also worried that she wouldn't come back. He had no idea what she had left behind when she had shown up with a car full of belongings, but he knew it was foolish to think she didn't have a whole life back in Miami. Even with her immediate family gone, she must have had friends and other relatives, a promising career, and perhaps a significant other. Now that she'd had time to get back on her feet a little, would she want to go back? Would she find her life in the city enticing again compared to her quiet life at the river? He just didn't know.

It would help if she told him when she was planning on returning. The last time he'd talked to her, she'd been unsure. He knew she must have a lot to get settled there but her drive to get to the bottom of the accident that took her family seemed to consume her. He feared that she could never let it go, that there would never be answers that would satisfy her, and that it would eventually tear her away from him.

After she told him about the accident, he had investigated a little on his own. He'd found several newspaper articles referring to the tragedy, and the headlines had been shocking: *Famous Lawyer, Family, Perish In Fiery Tragedy Aboard Yacht.* The articles had mentioned Kennedy, and many had focused on her absence aboard the boat that night. One read: *authorities are now questioning why Klark's daughter, Kennedy, also a lawyer, had not been on board, as she was listed on the float plan Klark had filed with the marina the evening before.* The news coverage had been relentless. As he read about it, his heart went out to her; it must have been terrible to come under such scrutiny in the wake of such a horrible event. But the last headline really tugged at him: *Daughter Of Wealthy Attorney Killed in Fiery Boat Accident Vanishes.* He had not realized she had come from such a prominent and wealthy family and that her dad, a well-known figure in law, was worthy of such media attention, but he understood now why she had fled. He also realized how hard it must have been for her to go back there.

The last time he'd talked to her, she had planned to see the estate attorney, and he was hoping she had gotten some things put to rest. He hadn't heard from her since, but he was hoping she would call him this evening, give him an update on things, and tell him when she was coming home. Certainly, by now, she would know.

The trips to the hunt camp were something he looked forward to a few times a year to reconnect with his friends and his military buddies. It usually meant a few days of hunting, good meals together, whiskey drinking, and a lot of camaraderie. Though it was not deer season, there were plenty of wild hogs to hunt year round. They were a dangerous and destructive nuisance on the property, and though hunting them was fun, the culling was also necessary. Controlling the ever-exploding population was nearly an impossible task.

He always came home from the camp feeling tired but renewed in his soul from sharing time with friends. This time, he felt slightly unsettled about being away for a few days. The nagging feeling he had in his gut about Kennedy had him distracted and preoccupied. He knew he would not rest until she was home.

The hunt camp consisted of 375 acres up in the panhandle of Florida near the Georgia line. When his friend, Jake, had bought the property nearly ten years before, after they were back from overseas, it had been a raw, wild property consisting of hardwood forests, a large natural lake, and a lot of slash pine. In the time since, helped by Gabe and friends, the acreage had been transformed into a pristine hunting property with groomed trails, planted fields, and a pretty cabin on the meadow by the lake. To say it was picturesque didn't do it justice.

Because of their close friendship, Jake always reserved the bunk room in the cabin for Gabe. Though he would have gladly camped in the meadow with the rest of the men, he knew Jake wouldn't have it. The two men had stayed up talking many nights in the cabin after the others had gone to bed. Over the years, the group of men gathered there primarily consisted of fellow veterans and several corrections officers from the state prison in Franklin, friends of Jake's, a unit manager there. To say they were a close group was an understatement, but Jake and Gabe had been members of the same Navy Seal Team and had a bond that superseded any other among the men.

The drive to the hunt camp through the back roads of North Florida was peaceful and beautiful. Now that they were into early summer, the crops planted in the spring were flourishing, and with the rain from the recent storm and rainy season upon them, everything was green and tall. With a little luck, it looked like the North Florida farmers might have a bumper crop this year.

Gabe pulled down the long, narrow, one-lane entrance into the property, and upon arriving at the campsite, he could see several guys had set up their tents and were getting settled. As he was parking the truck, he saw Jake come out of the cabin and down the front steps to talk to the guys standing around the central fire pit. When he saw Gabe walking over from his truck, he waved and motioned him over. The two men smiled as they shook hands and pulled each other into a bear hug. It had been a few weeks since they had seen each other.

"Hey man," Jake said with a smile, "I'm glad you're here."

"Glad to be here," Gabe said. "It's been a while, brother."

"Come on up to the cabin. Let's get you settled. Then we can join these knuckleheads for a drink before dinner."

It was the tradition that the men would cook steaks on the grill and roast potatoes in the fire pit on the first night of camp. When they were ready to eat, they would pile into the two large picnic tables and have their meal family style, enjoying being together and looking forward to the next few days of hunting and communing. Afterward, they would sit around the fire pit, drink whiskey, and swap stories and insults. It was a night that everyone looked forward to, a chance to unwind from the stresses of everyday life and gear up for the days ahead together. Tomorrow night they would eat an early dinner and head out after dark to hunt the hogs. They would hunt well into the night, taking them down and loading them into the back of the ATVs for disposal. Though it would be a raucous time, there would be no whiskey until the men were back at camp and had secured the guns.

As Gabe and Jake rejoined the group and the men began their few days together, Gabe felt grateful for his friends and their camaraderie. It lifted his heart to have the companionship of the men to lean on. These times helped him the most. Being with these men without the savages of war helped replace the bad memories with good ones. Still, he couldn't help checking his phone for messages from Kennedy. It was getting well into the evening, and he still had not heard from her.

After dinner, as Gabe settled into one of the camp chairs around the fire pit, Jake handed him a whiskey, and the two men raised their glasses to each other in a silent toast. With their bellies full, they were content to sit for a while, admire the fire and listen to the crickets and the frogs.

"So, how are things up at the farm, Gabe?" Jake asked." I know y'all got hit pretty hard by the storm. Everything get cleaned up ok?"

"Yeah, for the most part," Gabe said. "Everything is pretty much back to normal. I'm covered up with orders at the sawmill, though. Everybody wants their trees downed in the storm cut into lumber," he said as he chuckled.

"I'll bet," Jake said. "I can come over that way next week for a couple of days if you need some help. Just let me know."

"Thanks," Gabe said. "I may take you up on that."

The two men were quiet for a minute." How are things with you? How are Cindi and the girls?" Gabe asked.

"Good, good," Jake said with a smile. "Maybe I'll bring them up to the farm when I come. Those two little girls just love horses."

When Jake returned from overseas, he'd had a hard time like Gabe and most guys they served with. Cindi had been waiting for him, though, and he had been, with her help, able to assimilate back into everyday life slowly. Since then, Jake and Cindi had married and had children, and Gabe was happy that Jake had established a normal, happy life. Having the hunting camp to work on and spending a few days away here and there with Gabe and the guys had helped. It had helped them all feel normal again. Nobody other than the men who had been over there seemed to understand what it was like living with the memories. It was hard not to feel tense and on guard all the time and Gabe was sure that the ever-present vigilance would never leave him. It was with him even in sleep. Too many nights, he'd been awakened at the slightest noise and had gone door to door, window to window in the farmhouse to ensure everything was secure. Now that Kennedy was in his life, he hoped they could build a life together and that having someone to watch over and protect would help him put those feelings and impulses in their proper perspective.

"That would be great, Jake. I would love to see them and Cindi. We'll let the girls ride old Belle around. She hasn't moved any faster than a walk in years," Gabe said as he chuckled. They were silent for a few minutes again, watching the fire and listening to the quiet drone of the conversations of the other men.

"So," Jake said, "I ran into Finn in Franklin the other day. He tells me you have a woman in your life."

"That old bastard gets around, doesn't he?" Gabe laughed. "What did he say?"

"Just that she'd recently bought property up in the Oasis and that you two had been spending some time together. He seems to like her, says she's a good fit for you."

"Well, I think old Finn has been trying to play matchmaker, but he's right; she's a good fit for me," Gabe said as he took a sip of whiskey. "We've been taking it slow, but I think we're getting there. I've been working on opening up to her, but it's been hard. I haven't had a relationship with a woman in a long time, at least not a meaningful one. And she's coming off a terrible tragedy. Her immediate family was killed in a fire aboard their yacht in Miami not too long ago. That's why she's up here. She needed to get away. Her family, especially her father, was wealthy and well known, so the press coverage was relentless. She's also having a hard time accepting that it was an accident, and she has these ideas that her family was murdered. I think she's suffering from survivor's guilt because she was supposed to be with them when the accident happened. Honestly, Jake, I think I'm in love with this girl, but this obsession of hers could be a problem for us. I'm afraid I'm going to lose her over it."

Jake said nothing for a minute and his silence made Gabe turn and look at him. When he did, Jake was staring at him. "Where is she now, Gabe?"

"She's in Miami, wrapping up some stuff with her family's estate. Why?" Gabe asked.

"Gabe," Jake said without taking his eyes off him, "we've got an inmate in my unit up in Franklin who's been bragging to his cellmate that he knows some bad dudes in South Florida who carried out a hit on a wealthy family down there. We've been looking into it but haven't gotten very far. Gabe, he says they are trying to find the daughter they missed in the hit; they won't get paid unless they get her too. I think we are talking about the same thing. If she's in Miami, we gotta get her outta there."

Gabe felt his heart stop beating for a second and then felt his insides go cold. He and Jake immediately got up and ran toward the cabin. When they got through the door, Jake grabbed him by the arm.

"Listen, brother, we're gonna go get her, ok? I flew my Cessna up here from Franklin this afternoon. We're gonna fly down and snatch her outta there, you understand me? Now, get your stuff and meet me at my truck. Do you have your handgun and ammunition with you?"

"Of course," Gabe said as he struggled to slow down his heartbeats so he could breathe and think.

206

"Ok, grab my bag out of my room for me. I've got a couple of calls to make, and I'll meet you out there in a minute," he said as he started quickly dialing on his cell phone.

As Gabe waited for him in the truck, he tried calling Kennedy but got no answer, the call going to voicemail and ratcheting up his anxiety another notch. Moments later, he and Jake were barreling down the asphalt road toward the nearby grass strip, and within the hour, they were taking off into the night, airborne and bound for Miami.

When Kennedy looked at her watch, she was surprised to find it was an hour before midnight, much later than she realized. She packed the rest of the things she wanted to take with her and closed up the house again. As she passed through the kitchen, she noticed the keys to her Audi sports car on the counter by the house phone. In the days before she left for North Florida, she had purchased the Jeep to evade the press and have something more suitable for life in the woods and had left her Audi in the garage at her parent's house. Now, weeks later, she knew the car needed to be driven and decided to take it to the hotel and then to the river the next day.

She exited her parent's driveway through the security gates, stopping briefly to ensure they closed behind her. She wound around through the picturesque community of large homes, eventually pulling up to the guard house at the entrance. The guard inside smiled and waved as he raised the gate to let her through. As she made the right onto the boulevard, she thought she saw a flash of light in her rearview mirror, but when she watched for a minute, she saw nothing unusual.

It felt good to be behind the wheel of her Audi. Though she loved her Jeep, she'd missed the performance and comfort of the luxury sports car. It would be nice to drive it back to North Florida in the morning; its creature comforts would be welcome on the long drive.

The diary of her mother had been a complete surprise, but in reading a few pages, especially near the end, she had changed her entire perspective and view of her mother. Instead of the bitter aftertaste of rejection and criticism that had haunted her throughout her life, she now felt sympathy and understanding for her mother. She'd realized how her mother had become the person she was and what had shaped her as a mother. After hearing her grandmother recount her own childhood and her inadequacies as a mother, a lot of things fell into place for Kennedy. Somehow it was all weirdly comforting. She was grateful for her father, who had been there to love and nurture her. She was sure she would have been much more wounded by her mother's perceived indifference had he not been so affectionate and attentive.

As for the files on her father's computer and his letter to her, she still did not know what to make of it all, and finding Liam's laptop had been a surprise. There was so much to look through and analyze, and she was glad she'd been able to download the files onto flash drives so she could put the pieces together later. One thing she was sure of; these files had something to do with the murders of her family, and now that she knew that to be the case, the sooner she got out of Miami, the better.

She'd checked her phone before she left her parent's house and seen that Gabe had called twice. So engrossed in what she'd been doing, she hadn't noticed, and she felt bad she hadn't contacted him since yesterday morning. She'd meant to call him that afternoon, but since she'd stayed so late with her grandmother, she hadn't had a chance. Later in the day, she realized he was probably already at the hunt camp and didn't want to disturb his time there. Since she was heading back to the river early in the morning, she decided she would call him from the road.

As she pulled the Audi onto US-1 and headed for downtown, Kennedy noticed a car was following close behind her. Though she was not immediately alarmed, she kept her eye on it as they picked up speed and headed down the highway. The car kept pace with her, sitting behind her and maintaining an acceptable distance, so she relaxed a little. Because of the late hour, maneuvering through and around traffic was easy. When they got to a section with almost no cars, Kennedy noticed the vehicle behind her swing out and come alongside her. She would not have thought much about it had it not moved in so close to her. She moved over in her lane but quickly realized she had little room on that side. That part of the highway was under construction, and there was no shoulder, only a concrete barrier. She honked her horn to let the other driver know he was drifting over, but the vehicle kept coming. Looking ahead, she realized that the lane was ending, and the Audi was headed for a concrete barricade. In a split-second decision she hit the brakes hard and swung left, just missing the car's bumper by inches as she crossed nearly three lanes. The car that had tried to run her off the road sped forward, narrowly missing the barricade itself. She saw an on-ramp to I-95 to her left, and although she was going at a high rate of speed, she took it, the high-performance Audi handling the risky maneuver easily. If she'd been in the Jeep, she'd have been dead. She put the accelerator to the floor and headed for her downtown exit. Because she knew downtown Miami so well, she felt sure she could get to her hotel through the streets without being followed.

As the Cessna touched down at the executive airport in Miami, Gabe felt like he was going to come out of his skin. Even though they had a car waiting to pick them up, he'd felt like everything was happening in slow motion. Once on the ground, he'd called Kennedy's cell number, and it again had gone to voicemail, making his heart sink and his anxiety level heighten. He called her hotel, too, but when they put his call through to her room, there was no answer.

The Uber took them to Miami International Airport, where they rented a car. They had decided not to take her back to the river right away, at least until they could assess the ability of anyone to find her there. Instead, once they had her, Gabe would head north with her in the rental car, and Jake would clean up things in Miami. As they sped toward downtown, Gabe checked the time and saw it was 11 pm. Where could she be at this hour? They had requested hotel security check her room, but she was not there. With no idea where else she could be, all they could do was stake out her hotel, hoping to catch her when she came in, if she came in.

Jake dropped Gabe off at the entrance to the hotel and pulled the car south down Brickell over the bridge where he could wait for them. There was no way to do a curbside snatch near the hotel without someone noticing. Gabe carried a small bag stuffed with a hooded jacket and cased the hotel lobby looking for the fastest exit, other than the front entrance, to get back to Brickell without being seen. When he had a plan, he used the house phone to call her room again to make sure they hadn't missed each other somehow. There was no answer. All he could do was wait.

He settled into a quiet corner of the lobby, where he had a good view of the circular drive and the valet. With the approach of each set of headlights, he prayed that it was her. As time passed, he felt more and more discouraged. Suddenly he saw a tall, dark-haired woman get out of a white Audi that had pulled further around the driveway and parked directly in front of the valet stand. While he'd been looking for the Jeep, his heart skipped a beat when he saw her. As she turned, he recognized her profile, and an overwhelming sense of relief flooded through him. But, what caught his attention was the fear on her face. Something had happened.

He readied himself near the entrance, and when she stepped through it, he gently called her name, not wanting to frighten her. When she turned and saw him, he saw a range of emotions on her face, from disbelief to confusion, but she did not hesitate and came toward him, grasping his outstretched hand. He turned immediately and headed for the restaurant to the left of the main lobby. Though it was late, the bar was still open, and they could slither through the dark interior to the side doors that led out to a patio along the river. There they could turn right alongside the hotel, then turn left and go over the bridge on the footpath to the other side where Jake was waiting. Once outside, he stopped, pulled the hooded jacket from the bag, put it on her, and dialed his phone.

"I've got her," he said, "headed your way." He disconnected and turned to her.

"Give me your shoes," he said. She didn't question him to her credit as she wrestled off her sling-backs and handed them to him. Gabe stuffed them in the bag and then put the bag in a trash can that sat near the entrance to the hotel. He pulled the hood over her head, slung her bag over his shoulder, and looked her in the eyes. "You ready?" he said. She nodded, and he said, "Ok, let's go."

They walked briskly toward Brickell to the end of the walk, then turned left and started over the bridge. While Gabe's outward demeanor remained casual, the soldier in him was wildly vigilant, his eyes darting around like a madman's. When they reached the crest of the bridge, a dark car came speeding past them, headed for the hotel, and Kennedy turned to Gabe.

"That's them," she whispered.

With that, Gabe stepped up the pace, and as they started down the other side of the bridge, he waved to Jake to come. As Jake pulled the car out onto Brickell, Gabe looked over his shoulder but, to his relief, saw no cars coming after them. When Jake pulled up alongside them, Gabe yanked the back door open, pushed Kennedy in, and was inside before Jake ever came to a stop. As they sped down Brickell and passed the front of the hotel, Gabe saw the car and two men get out and head inside. He'd gotten there just in time.

When they felt they were far enough away from the hotel, Jake pulled over, got out, and turned the car over to Gabe.

"Kennedy," Gabe said, "give me your room key and valet ticket." She fished around in her bag and handed both over the seat to Gabe, who was now in the driver's seat. He handed them out the window to Jake.

"I'm going to circle back to the hotel," Jake said. "What's your room number, Kennedy?"

"2310," she said, her voice a little weak.

"I'm going to see if I can get a bead on these guys. I'll let things cool off there for a while, then I'll clean out her room. I've got some backup coming. We are going to end this thing here. Keep in touch, brother, stay safe, and I'll see you soon." Jake said.

"Thank you, Jake," Gabe said as he grasped the man's hand through the window. "I'll never be able to repay you for tonight."

"You paid in advance a long time ago, brother," Jake said as he turned, walked away, and disappeared into the night.

Chapter Fifteen

Be strong and courageous. Do not be afraid or terrified because of them, for the LORD your God goes with you; he will never leave you nor forsake you.
Deuteronomy 31:6

G abe sped north on I-95, trying to put Miami in his rearview mirror quickly. It had been too close. He had come too close to losing her, and he'd be damned if he would ever let that happen again.

She had not asked him questions but had stared straight ahead into the night into the oncoming headlights for a while. Finally, in the rearview mirror, he'd seen her head roll back against the seat and her eyes close as the fatigue and the after-effects of the adrenaline had set in. He was glad to see her rest. There would be plenty of time for questions later.

He was mad at himself, furious. When she told him she thought someone had murdered her family, he'd brushed it off, thinking she was having a hard time adjusting to the loss. Looking back, he should have known to trust her instincts. She had wickedly accurate intuition, and she was exceptionally smart.

He set his cell phone and the burner phone Jake had given him on the dash so he wouldn't miss any calls, though he didn't expect any for the next few hours. He needed to focus on getting her to a safe location which, by his calculation, was still about two and half hours away. Where he was taking her, he was sure no one could find her.

At four-thirty in the morning, Gabe exited I-95 and headed east toward the little beach town. Kennedy roused and looked out the window as if detecting the change in speed and direction.

"Where are we?" she said in a soft, sleepy voice. Gabe didn't answer, and when their eyes met in the mirror, she seemed to understand that she needed to trust him and not ask questions. He drove slowly through the heart of town, minding the speed limit, then turned left onto A1A, heading north along the beach. Kennedy noticed that the houses became sparser, and the space between them grew longer as they traveled along the coastline. Finally, Gabe slowed and pulled into a shell driveway that sloped down and curved to the right in front of a stately old beach house.

They sat for a minute, both relieved to be at their destination. Kennedy looked expectantly at Gabe in the mirror, and he got out of the car and opened the door to the back seat. She slid over and took his hand, and righted herself on her feet. She felt a little disoriented, and as if he knew, he pulled her in close to him and walked her to the door.

He fished around in his pocket for keys and, with one hand, opened the door. He let her go ahead, and as he entered, he switched on the lights that lit up the house in a soft glow. She didn't know exactly where he had taken her, but she knew it was somewhere that was familiar to him.

He put his arm around her and led her to a bedroom off the main room. While she stood there, he turned down the covers, arranged the pillows for her, then patted the bed, beckoning her to lie down. When she did, he covered her with the sheet and comforter, kissed her forehead, switched off the light, and left the room, leaving the door open. She lay there for a while, listening to him move about the house. She didn't know what he was doing, but she felt comforted by his presence and the sense he was watching over her and keeping her safe. Finally, she heard him switch off the light and lie down on the living room couch. She closed her eyes and was instantly drawn into sleep.

Gabe awoke with a start. He quickly realized where he was and that they were safe. The sun was up in the sky and streaming in the front windows that faced east. By his estimation, it was mid-morning.

He pulled his large frame off the couch and peeked in at Kennedy. She was still sound asleep; the covers pulled up under her chin in a pose that told him she felt safe. He pulled the door closed but not shut. He didn't think he could ever let her out of his sight again. He'd come too close to losing her.

He hadn't been to the beach house in more than a year; the obligations of the farm and his businesses had kept him away, it seemed. But honestly, the place had felt lonely to him since the last time he had been there with family. It was a house built for joyful children and family gatherings. Being alone there was depressing. But, now that he was there with Kennedy, the place had taken on a different feel that felt comforting and somewhat hopeful.

There wasn't much in the way of provisions in the house, nothing fresh. He could probably scrounge up something to eat out of the canned goods in the pantry, but they would have to head into town sooner than later. He found some coffee, made a pot, and took a cup out onto the front porch, where he waited for Kennedy to wake up.

Soon after, he heard the screen door open, and Kennedy walked out onto the porch, wrapped in the afghan draped across the end of her bed.

"Hi," she said as she sat next to him on the porch swing.

215

"Hi, yourself," Gabe said. "How are you feeling?"

"Like I have a hangover but somehow missed all the fun."

Gabe chuckled." Your sleep schedule is off. You'll feel better later."

"How is it that you…" she started to ask.

"Not now, Kennedy," he said, cutting her off. "I'll explain everything to you later."

She nodded and was quiet for a moment. "I have to say the last couple of days have been the weirdest of my life. If I tried, I couldn't make this stuff up," she said with a sigh.

"Tell me something weird," he said.

"Well, I have a grandmother that nobody ever told me about. I met her yesterday," she said, her voice quivering a little.

Gabe raised his eyebrows; he hadn't been expecting that. "Really?" he said. "What's she like?" Gabe asked the question to keep her talking, knowing she needed to process the events that had happened to her over the last few days.

"She's a lot like me, actually," Kennedy said, staring out at the blue waters of the Atlantic.

"In what way?" he asked.

"Well, we look a lot alike for one thing," she said, "but we think alike too. We've lived way different lives, but somehow we've ended up in the same place now."

"Really, how so?" he said, genuinely curious.

"We are all each other has," she said, her lip quivering again.

He reached over and pulled her to him, and they sat for a while, the swing barely rocking. It was enough for now. Better to let her process one thing at a time.

A little while later, he heard the ping of his burner phone. He checked it and read the message:

Hotel room clean. Will deliver the Audi.

Kennedy was still sitting on the porch swing, and he thought it was probably good to let her be alone with her thoughts for a few minutes. He knew there was a lot more to know about her trip to Miami, and some of it would be tough to deal with. The look on her face when he'd first seen her at the hotel meant that something had happened that had frightened her. Just that would be enough to shell shock her for a while. It would take some time for her to work through and process everything. Pressuring her now for any information was the wrong thing to do. He sat and listed grocery items they would need for the next few days. Until he knew it was safe to take her home, they would stay put.

"I found some clothes that were left here, just some shorts and t-shirts if you want to shower and change," Gabe said as he returned to the porch. "There are plenty of clean towels and some toiletries in the bathroom if you need anything."

"Thank you," she said, smiling at him." I was just trying to figure out how I would manage all that."

As she passed him and headed for the bedroom, he felt terrible for keeping things from her. But it was better that she not know much detail about things. Until he heard from Jake about what he'd been able to discover or what had been taken care of down there, it was best she be kept in the dark. While Gabe didn't know Jake's plan, he had a good idea. If these guys had killed Kennedy's family and were after her, their days on this planet were numbered. That's how it worked on the dark side. He knew. He'd walked in that world.

When she was showered and dressed, she went to the living area where Gabe was resting in a chair, his eyes closed. She didn't know if he was sleeping, so she quietly sat down on the couch, not wanting to disturb him.

"How was your shower?" he asked, opening one eye.

"I guess nobody ever sneaks up on you, do they?" she said with a laugh.

"Not if I can help it," he said with a smile. "Do you feel up to going into town? We could use some groceries. I called an order in, so we just need to pick it up."

"Sure," she said. "I'm pretty hungry. Can we get lunch too?"

"I can pick something up for us while we are out. I don't think it's a good idea for you to be out in public right now, not until we know more."

"Oh," she said. "I could just stay here while you go then."

"Nope," he said. "I'm not leaving you alone here. I'm afraid you are stuck with me for a while."

———

Kennedy sat at the kitchen island drinking wine while Gabe cooked them dinner. He was happy to see her relax, and she seemed to return to herself somewhat. The conversation was lighthearted, a nice change from the stress of the last couple of days.

"Tell me about this house," she said, looking around. "Looks to be late 40's architecture?"

218

"Yep," he said. "You're dead on. My granddad built it in 1948, back when there was nothing on this beach. It was just a sleepy little village, and down here on the north end, there were no houses, in fact, there was nothing between town and the lighthouse. He bought the land dirt cheap and spent a few years building it. It was the only house out here for a long time. He was smart and bought up the land on either side too so there would never be any close neighbors. I grew up coming here with my family and cousins. When my grandad passed, he left it to my dad. And when my parents passed, it was left to my sister and me, but she lives in Canada now and had no interest in it. So now it's mine, and unfortunately, I rarely get over here."

"Why don't you come here more often? It's so beautiful here," she asked.

"Oh, I don't know. The farm and the business keep me pretty busy, and, honestly, it's not much fun to be here alone. My friend Jake comes with his family for a couple of weeks every summer. I'm just happy that someone gets to enjoy it, especially the kids."

"Well, I think you should come more often. It's a nice change from the river, and I think it's just lovely," she said. "And whatever you're making over there smells divine. I didn't know you were such a good cook."

"Hey," he said. "I cooked for you at Finn's."

"You did, and it was delicious, but apparently, you have more skill than I realized. That's chicken piccata, isn't it?"

"It is," he said, smiling at her, "and it's almost ready."

After dinner, they took their wine out to the porch swing, where they could listen to the waves and stargaze. The night sky was cloudless, and the nearly full moon was high in the sky, making the scene picturesque. Kennedy felt like she was finally decompressing from the events in Miami, though the mystery surrounding her brother was much on her mind. She was eager to look at the files and try to piece together what Liam was involved in. Whatever it was, her dad was on to it, though it was clear he hadn't figured it all out before he died. He had charged her with that task, and she was ready to do it.

She wanted to know what Gabe knew. He had discovered something, or he wouldn't have come to Miami looking for her. She knew he was trying to protect her by letting her come down slowly from the trauma of the events, but he should give her some answers.

"Let's play a game," she said.

"What kind of game?" he said.

"I tell you something interesting; then you do the same."

"Ok," he said. "You go first."

She took a deep breath, and he sensed she was ready to talk about things. He would have preferred to wait a little longer, let more time pass, and talk to Jake, but he could tell he couldn't put her off any longer.

"My father left me a letter in a secret drawer in his office; I found it when I went to my parent's house last night," she said matter of factly. Gabe's eyebrows lifted; he could have never guessed that one.

"What did the letter say?" he asked.

"No, that's not how the game works. Now you have to tell me something interesting. We go back and forth. See?"

Gabe nodded and contemplated what he wanted to tell her. He was quiet for a minute.

"I found out you were right about your family. I'm sorry, I should have trusted your instincts," he said. She nodded and let that statement rest while she thought about what she wanted to say next.

"My father thought my brother was mixed up in something bad, and he left me the letter in case something happened to him," she said, her voice cracking ever so slightly. Gabe reached over and took her hand, entwining his fingers in hers.

"Your turn," she said quietly.

He paused again, trying to tell her as little as possible. "I came to Miami because I thought you were in danger," he said trying to hedge a little.

"That's cheating; that's obvious," she said. "Try again."

He knew he would not get away with pandering to her. She was too smart for that. And, as much as he wanted to end the game, he needed to know what she had uncovered.

"Jake says there's an inmate up in Franklin who may know something about what happened to your family," he said.

That made her pause for a minute. He knew she must have questions about that one, but she was abiding by the rules of the game and wasn't asking.

"Your turn," he said

"My dad had some encrypted files on his computer; the keys to them were in the letter, and I downloaded them, but I don't know what's in them yet," she said and then took a deep breath." Now you go."

Gabe was quiet for a minute, then turned to her. "I think we should stop playing games and talk for a bit. There's a lot more for each of us to know about what's happened," he said as he studied her face. She nodded, and he went on. "It was purely by divine intervention that I found out about the inmate. God was looking out for us, Kennedy. I was having a casual conversation with Jake at the hunt camp, and he asked about you. I told him what had happened to your family and that you were struggling with reconciling how it happened. He put two and two together, and from what this guy had said, they were looking for you. We knew it was just a matter of time before they figured out you were in Miami and that we had to get you out of there."

"How did you get down there so fast?" she asked.

"Jake has a plane that he flew to the hunt camp. There's a grass strip not far away. We flew into Miami, got a car, and went to your hotel. We got there not long before you did. I was frantic, Kennedy. I'd been calling your hotel and cell phone, but you weren't answering," he said.

She squeezed his hand. "I'm sorry," she said. "I didn't mean to be out of touch. I spent the whole day with my grandmother yesterday, and by the time I was on my way to my parent's house, I figured you were already at the hunt camp, and I didn't want to bother you. Once I was at the house, I was super busy trying to get everything done so I could leave to go home today. I wasn't checking my phone at all. And then, with what happened on the way back to the hotel, I haven't even looked at it since yesterday evening."

"It's ok," he said. "I'm just so thankful we got there when we did. Can you tell me what happened on the way to the hotel?"

"They tried to run me off the road into a concrete barrier," she said. "It was the car that we saw at the hotel. It started following me when I left my parent's house. I'd decided to take my Audi. When I realized what was happening, I just reacted and thank God the Audi could handle it. If I'd been in the Jeep, I'd be dead right now."

He put his arm around her, pulled her over close to him, and she laid her head on his shoulder. They sat there for a long while, gently swinging and listening to the waves. That was enough for the night. When he realized she was dozing off, he gently untangled himself from her and pulled her carefully to her feet. When she was tucked away in bed, he resumed his position on the couch in the living room not far from her door. Again, he wanted to lie down next to her, not for anything other than to be close to her, but he would not do that until she asked him to.

Gabe was suddenly awake. He lay still and listened. He heard the faint but distinctive sound of footsteps, but he knew they were not from Kennedy moving around her room. He could tell they were coming from outside the house. He reached for his gun on the coffee table, got up, and walked silently to Kennedy's door. Seeing she was asleep, he closed her door and checked his watch. It was four-fifteen. He moved toward the front door with the stealth of a jaguar, by instinct, due to his Seal training. Carefully pulling back the sheer curtain on the highlight window to the left of the front door, he saw nothing that looked askew. Under other circumstances, he would have exited through the beachside door and made his way through the heavy brush around the side of the house to the front, but he did not want to leave Kennedy alone in the house. He moved to the kitchen to see if he could see anyone from the window but saw nothing moving about in the moonlight. As he moved around from window to window, he saw no one, but he was sure he had heard the footsteps and something had awakened him. Someone was there.

Just then, he heard the ping of his burner phone. He fished it out of his pocket and shielded the screen so it wouldn't produce a light that might draw attention. It was a short text:

Here. Back Porch.

In case it was a ploy, he stuck the gun in the back of his jeans. He carefully and silently moved to the window overlooking the back porch and saw Jake sitting in the chair closest to the door. He unlocked the door and stepped out.

"Hey, brother," Jake said as he got up from the chair. The two men clasped hands and pulled each other into a hug. "Are you guys doing ok? How is she?"

"Yeah, we are ok. She's doing better than expected. This thing is complicated. What were you able to find out? What happened down there?"

"Well, the less you know, the better, but I think this was a one-off thing. I don't think she has anything to worry about now."

"Really? She thinks her brother may have been mixed up with some bad people. How do we know someone else won't come after her?"

"The idiots, and believe me, they were idiots, weren't real professionals; they were street rats," Jake said. "They said the guy who hired them hasn't been in touch for quite a while. They thought he was long gone by now, probably out of the county 'cause they never got paid the rest of their money. After they hit the family on the boat, they figured the situation was too hot for him to hang around. When they realized she wasn't on the boat, they thought that's why he didn't pay up the other half. The gig was to take out the whole family with the fire, so they figured they had to get her to get paid. They never had any direct contact with him. This wasn't a professional hit, Gabe, in my opinion."

"Why is the question, Jake, why would someone want to take out a whole family?" Gabe asked.

"My opinion? This whole thing was a cover for something. They got lucky with the boat fire. That amateur move should have failed. The whole thing was sloppy."

"Where are they now?" Gabe asked.

"That's for me to know, brother, and you to never know," Jake said. "Anyway, her Audi is here, and her stuff from the hotel is in the trunk. Give me the keys to the rental car. I'll take it back to Miami and then fly home. I think this thing is over."

"Thank you, Jake. You always did finish a mission well."

"What mission?" he asked. "You and I spent the weekend deep sea fishing, right, brother?" Jake smiled and gave Gabe a wink and in a quick minute, he was gone.

When Kennedy woke up, the sun coming through her bedroom windows was bright, even through the curtains. When she looked out the window, she saw the sun rising in the eastern sky in a brilliant collage of heavenly colors. She peeked out the door, but Gabe was not on the sofa. She could see him through the windows to the porch sitting on the porch swing, watching the sunrise. She wondered if the man ever slept.

She poured herself a cup of coffee and headed out to join him. When she stepped through the door, he turned and smiled at her, and when she sat beside him, he took her hand, but they didn't speak for a while. They watched the sunrise and the blue waters until the sun was up in the sky. Finally, Gabe turned to her.

"Feel like a walk?" he asked.

"Yes," she said. "That sounds good."

"Where is your phone?"

"In my bag, still," she said. "Why?"

225

"Can you get it for me?" Confused, she went in, found her phone in the bottom of her tote, and brought it to him.

"It's almost dead," she said, thinking he wanted to use it for something,

"That's ok," he said as he took the phone and set it next to his and the burner phone on the kitchen counter. He grabbed her hand and led her out the screen door onto the porch. They walked down the front steps and onto the sand for about a hundred feet, then over the dunes and down to the beach. They turned north toward the old lighthouse, standing stately on the point by the inlet, its form lit up bright white by the morning sun. When they had walked a little way down the beach he turned to her and put his hands on her shoulders.

"Kennedy, I want you to know that you no longer have to fear the men who took the lives of your family and tried to run you off the road. Don't ask me any questions about it, but I wanted you to know that they are no longer a threat to you. Do you understand?" she nodded, and he went on.

"As to why it happened, we don't know, but we feel pretty confident that whoever hired these men is gone, probably out of the country. I don't think that person will risk sticking their head up again. Going after you was an afterthought because you weren't on the boat. Now that the hired men are...gone...I think it's over. I really think it's over, Kennedy."

She took a deep breath and looked up at the sky. "What about my dad's letter? And the files he left?" she asked. "Gabe, I have to get to the bottom of that. I can't believe that it's unrelated. What if my brother was involved in something really bad? My dad said money was involved, lots of money. What if whomever my brother was mixed up with did this? Won't they just send someone else after me?"

226

Gabe thought for a minute. "It just doesn't make sense for them to come after you. You weren't involved in any of that; you don't have any knowledge of anything that could hurt them. Jake said he felt like this was a cover for something, and the men told him the person who hired them to set the fire didn't seem experienced in this kind of thing. I agree it feels related, but this was not a professional hit, Kennedy."

"I don't know, Gabe," she said," I really don't, but my dad wanted me to figure this thing out, so that's what I'm going to do. I've got the files, and I also found Liam's laptop in the carriage house at my parent's house, where he'd been living. I think if there are answers to be found, I can find them there."

Gabe nodded and put his arm around her. He had thoughts on the matter but now was not the time to share them. They walked a little further, then turned around and headed back toward the house. Now that the immediate threat was gone, they could return to the river anytime, but he hoped they could stay on for a couple of days. It would be nice to relax with her and enjoy some downtime. He didn't know if she would agree, but he hoped to convince her. Without the pressures of the world closing in on them, they might cement things between them. He was finally ready.

Chapter Sixteen

"From their callous hearts comes iniquity; their evil imaginations have no limits." Psalms 73:7

G abe navigated the Audi along the scenic coastline toward the little beach town. Evening was settling in, and the shoreline was a beautiful shade of pink, the remnants of the sunset casting a rosy glow onto the white sand and the foamy crests of the waves. As beautiful as the hour before nightfall was, it had always cast a bittersweet melancholy across his soul. Now, being there with Kennedy, it felt different. He couldn't say exactly how. It just did.

They had spent the day enjoying the good weather, swimming in the temperate ocean, and lying on the sand. It had been relaxing and therapeutic for them both, and when they had ended their day with a glass of wine on the porch, freshly showered and changed, he realized he could not have imagined a more perfect day.

Instead of cooking, he took her to the little town's oldest and best restaurant. The small building that had always been its home was classic old Florida with its bungalow style and batten board siding. Built in the early 1900s, it had weathered the sea air and the ravages of time with grace. It wasn't anything fancy, but the food was good, and the owners were always friendly and accommodating. Gabe and his family had been going there since he was a young boy, and, in at least the last three decades, nothing had changed about the place.

They were seated at a quiet table in the corner and ordered a bottle of wine while waiting for their food. The smells and sounds of the place were comforting to Gabe, and though it had been some time since he'd been there, it felt a little bit like coming home.

"Now that things have settled down," Gabe said, " we can head back to the river any time you want."

"I've been thinking about that," she said. "When do you want to go?"

"Well," he said. "I was hoping we could stay a couple more days. It would be nice to just relax a little here with you. But I know you are probably eager to get home, so if you want to head back tomorrow, we can."

She thought about that for a minute. "Staying here for a couple of days with you sounds nice," she said. "I think I'd like to do that."

He smiled at her, noticing her beautiful features were touched with a hint of pink from the sun and the sea. It felt good to finally be honest about things between them. He hoped these next couple of days would keep the momentum of their relationship going. It seemed like they were both ready to acknowledge and move forward with what was between them.

Just then, the waitress delivered their food, and they feasted on Florida spiny lobster stuffed with crab and fresh shrimp. It was the perfect meal to end such a special day. Gabe hoped that with their relationship solidifying, there would be many more like this.

As they wound down dinner, Kennedy seemed to grow quiet and reflective. Gabe knew that she would have her highs and lows coming down off the last few days, but he had hoped to keep her distracted, at least tonight.

"You ok?" he asked.

"Yes," she said, "just thinking,"

"About?" he asked.

She paused for a minute, then asked, "What, if anything, do you know about hacking a laptop?"

Gabe's eyebrows shot up; he wasn't expecting that question.

"I know a little," he said. "What are you thinking?"

"I need to get into Liam's computer; I was hoping you might be able to help me."

Gabe knew a lot about hacking computers. As a Seal with a degree in IT that had been one of his specialties. He hadn't done it in a long time but remembered a lot. He knew that sometimes getting into a machine was a matter of understanding the obvious about its owner, which left him at a disadvantage since he hadn't known Liam. He would need to ask her lots of questions.

"I can try to help," he said, " but no guarantees."

Back at the beach house, they shared a nightcap on the porch swing and chatted until it was apparent Kennedy was ready for sleep, her head on his shoulder and her eyes closed. He tried to do this every night so she would be spared the time before sleep when everything in the world seemed to rush in. He knew good sleep would be an essential part of her healing.

When he had tucked her in, like he had done every night since they had gotten to the beach house, Gabe was restless. Even though he should have been exhausted from the lack of sleep over the last few days, he didn't feel tired enough to lie down. He had a restlessness in his bones and knew what it was. He had a question in his mind that needed an answer, and he knew he would not rest until he'd found it.

When Kennedy had asked him to help her access her brother's computer, he'd known what to do. He'd asked her fundamental questions about Liam that might make guessing the password easier. But if he couldn't crack it, there were other ways. He would get in eventually.

He pulled the laptop from Kennedy's bag and noticed the handgun in the bottom. The sight of it reminded him of the danger she had been in. Would she have been able to defend herself if she'd needed to? He just didn't know, and the thought of it wrenched his insides.

He set the laptop on the table in front of him and opened it. He knew from his training that most passwords were easy to guess. He'd tried to glean enough information from Kennedy about her brother to give it a try, but he wasn't necessarily hopeful. He started with the basics and the typically predictable passwords but with no luck. He'd then gone down the list of things in his head he had asked her, methodically crossing off possibilities in his head. When he typed in BMWM850, the car Liam drove, suddenly the computer logged on, and he was in.

For the next few hours, he went through the files, emails, and texts on Liam's laptop. Because he had synced up his phone with his computer, it provided a mirror image of his texts and phone calls. At a few minutes until five, he shut the computer and slipped it back into Kennedy's bag. He had his answer. Now the question was how and when to tell her.

———

A few hours later, when he opened his eyes, Kennedy was up and in the kitchen making coffee. He sat up and stretched, his back feeling the effect of nights spent on the couch. He needed coffee as the sleep deprivation was getting to him. He'd only had a few hours of sleep over the last three days, and he felt the weight of the fatigue in his joints. When he'd been overseas, long periods without sleep had been the norm, but now that he was a little older, he didn't seem to handle it as well.

Coffee on the porch had become their morning ritual, much like at the river. If they were up early enough, they would watch the sun rise over the water and slowly turn the sky from white-hot, yellow and orange to a soothing calm blue tone. The white sugar sand offered up the perfect contrast to the aqua-colored water creating a picturesque scene that looked like a painting on canvas. Because there were few houses on the north end of the beach, there were almost no people to be seen, save for the occasional jogger or lonely walker. He could have sat there all day with her, but he'd planned to take her out to lunch and to see some of the area. He didn't want her feeling cooped up at the house.

They had been quiet for a while, watching the sandpipers and gulls chase the tide back and forth and listening to the ebb and flow of the gentle surf. The offshore breeze they had enjoyed for the last few days had shifted, so the waves were small, and the sea beyond them was flat calm.

"Not to bug you," she said, " but do you think you might be able to take a look at the laptop today?"

Gabe said nothing right away. He hadn't planned on this. He'd hoped she would put it off, and he would have more time to figure out exactly how to show her what he'd found. But he knew that if Kennedy was anything, she was determined. Charged with a mission, she would go after it. He understood that because they had that in common.

He realized she was looking at him, her expression a questioning one. He couldn't lie to her, and there was nothing he could say that would be honest other than telling her the truth.

"I already have," he said, not taking his eyes off the blue water.

"Really?" she said. "When?"

"Last night, after you went to bed."

"And?" she said expectantly.

"I was able to get in," he said quietly.

"That's great, can you show me?"

He hesitated. What he was about to show her was devastating, and even though he had suspected it since his conversation with Jake, it was still a shock when he discovered the evidence that confirmed it. She had no idea what was coming, and he feared it was too soon, but he realized there was nothing he could do to stop her now.

"Kennedy," he said gently, "what I found on the laptop isn't good. And it won't make a difference if you see it now or later. I just think it would be better to…"

"Listen, Gabe," she said, cutting him off, "I know you are trying to protect me, and I appreciate that, I really do. But I'm a big girl, and this is important to me. Whatever is on that computer about my brother, I can handle. It probably won't surprise me. Will you please just show me?"

He got up and went inside, with her following him close behind. He retrieved the laptop from her bag and set it on the coffee table again. He stopped and looked at her, but from the determined look on her face, he knew he could stall no longer. With a sigh, he opened it.

"Luckily, Liam wasn't very creative with his password," he said as he typed it in, and the desktop full of icons appeared. "There is a lot on here, Kennedy, but I duplicated some files and took snapshots of a few things for you and put them in a folder here on the desktop."

"Ok," she said a little breathlessly.

With reluctance, he pushed the laptop over in front of her and noticed her hands were shaking ever so slightly as she worked the glide pad, opening the folder. As she clicked on the files and snapshots and browsed through them, he braced himself for the moment she would realize the truth. Suddenly, her head snapped around, and her eyes found his, searching for an explanation for what she saw. She tried to speak but couldn't find her voice. Finally, she shook her head, and her eyes filled with tears.

"I don't understand; how could this be? What does this mean?" she asked, unable to comprehend what she what she had just seen.

Gabe put his arms around her and held her for a minute. When he released her, he put his hands on her shoulders and looked her in the eyes. Slowly he said the words that her brain was desperately trying to grasp.

"Liam ordered the hit, Kennedy, and he is still alive."

Epilogue

When he checked his watch, he realized it was only a little past ten in the morning. Not that it should have surprised him since this day wasn't much different from any other. The bartender at the beach bar had long since stopped asking him what he was drinking or if he wanted a refill and instead kept them coming until Liam threw a wad of cash on the bar and staggered away. Somehow, he thought his life would be different from this.

It had been too easy. The money seemed to be there for the taking, and for a long time, he kidded himself into thinking no one would ever know. Not the clients, not his father. It had started as a little here and there, but after he met her, it had gotten out of hand. She was accustomed to a lavish and expensive lifestyle, and he'd had to skim more and more money to keep her happy and satisfied. But as things unraveled, he realized there was only one way out. The client had started asking questions, and his dad had been poking around. Since last year, when he started spending large amounts of money and transferring the rest offshore, he could tell his dad had been suspicious. He'd constantly been on his case about his lifestyle, spending habits, and lack of responsibility. The last straw had been when he'd thrown Liam's company credit card bill on his desk and demanded answers. It had been an ugly confrontation, and he had grown sick and tired of answering to his father for every little thing.

He had joined his father's firm when he graduated from law school because it had been the easy path. The firm was already very lucrative and somewhat famous, and he started with a big salary and a predetermined path to becoming a partner. His dad had been eager to make him into the mirror image of himself, but once Liam began the lifestyle his position afforded him, he lost interest in putting in the hard work his father expected from him. Instead, he found himself gratified only by the seemingly endless supply of women and drugs and the party lifestyle of living in Miami. He'd sometimes envied his sister for her choice not to join the firm, but he mostly just despised her and her goody-two-shoes persona.

Now that everyone thought he was dead and he was tucked away in this sleepy little beach village with all the money he could ever spend and then some, he should be happy. He hoped he'd pulled off the perfect scam and no one would ever come looking for him. He still owed the scum he had hired to torch the boat half of their money, but there was no way he would ever risk exposing himself by creating a trail back to them. Unfortunately, his sister hadn't been on the boat, but he wasn't worried about her. The lucky bitch had inherited a fortune. In his mind, that should be enough to keep her busy and happy and not wondering about her supposed-to-be-dead brother.

The Venezuelans he had stolen from were another matter. Even though he had buried the transactions that had yielded the stolen proceeds, he could not be sure someone would never find them. The shell game they had been playing to launder money was complicated, but he was afraid he might have become too greedy. If they ever suspected he was alive, they would never stop looking for him.

He obsessed over that thought day and night, constantly going over every detail of the plan in his head. When he was clear-headed and not high or drunk, which wasn't often, he reassured himself that he had covered everything. From the identities he'd established to the escape plan he'd put together to how he'd routed the money, he could not think of a single detail he had missed. Still, there were nights when he awoke in a cold sweat, sure that there was something he'd overlooked.

It was on one of those nights that he realized there was something he could not quite remember. He had packed hastily in his hurry to get to the boat that evening. He'd needed two bags. One to leave on the boat as evidence he was there and one to take with him when he escaped. It should have been in the bag that perished in the fire, destroying it forever, but no matter how hard he tried, he couldn't remember putting it there. If he hadn't, it would be the one thing that might lead someone to him. If his laptop ever fell into the wrong hands, he would be a dead man walking, and there would be no place on earth he could ever hide.

Coming Spring of 2023
The Road to Nowhere
Book Two in The Oasis Series

Made in United States
Orlando, FL
08 January 2023

28419582R00130